CW01370396

The Theory & Practice of Lunch

Also by Keith Waterhouse

THERE IS A HAPPY LAND

BILLY LIAR

JUBB

THE BUCKET SHOP

THE PASSING OF THE THIRD-FLOOR BUCK

BILLY LIAR ON THE MOON

MONDAYS, THURSDAYS

OFFICE LIFE

RHUBARB, RHUBARB

MAGGIE MUGGINS

IN THE MOOD

FANNY PECULIAR

MRS POOTER'S DIARY

THINKS

WATERHOUSE AT LARGE

THE COLLECTED LETTERS OF A NOBODY

Keith Waterhouse

The Theory & Practice of Lunch

MICHAEL JOSEPH · LONDON

First published in Great Britain by Michael Joseph Ltd

27 Wrights Lane, London W8
1986

© Keith Waterhouse Ltd. 1986
© in illustrations Thomas Boulton 1986

Illustrations by Thomas Boulton

All rights reserved. No part of this publication
may be reproduced, stored in a retrieval sytem,
or transmitted in any form or by any means,
electronic, mechanical, photocopying, recording
or otherwise, without the prior permission
of the Copyright owner

British Library Cataloguing in Publication Data

Waterhouse, Keith
 The theory and practice of lunch.
 1. Luncheons—Anecdotes, facetiae,
 satire, etc.
 I. Title
 394.1'5   GT2960

ISBN 0-7181-2781-1

Printed and bound in Great Britain by
Butler & Tanner, Frome

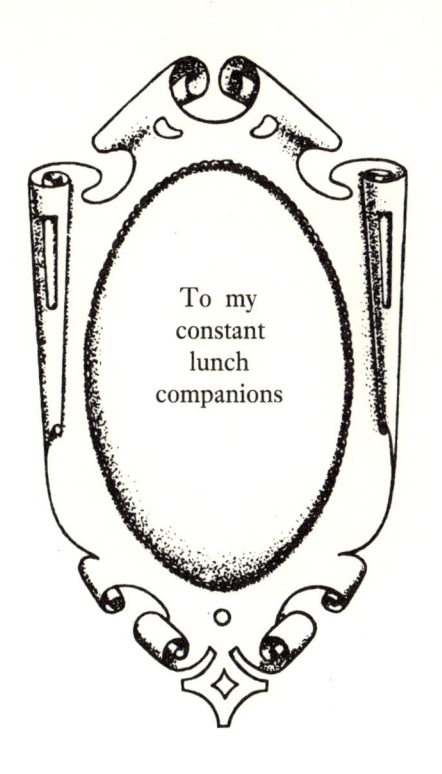

To my
constant
lunch
companions

The Menu

What this book is not / 1
Short history of lunch / 2
What lunch is not / 4
What lunch is / 7
Why lunch is not dinner / 9
Useful phrases / 11
Ambience / 12
Clutter / 16
Out places / 19
Duties of the lunch companion / 21
Table-hopping / 24
The menu / 27
The eating part / 32
Lemons / 36
A glass of water / 38
A nice salad / 41
Only if you will / 43
The drinking part / 45
Bad companions / 49
The bill / 52

The Menu

The tip / 55
Indigestifs / 59
Eating on t' street / 61
Brasseries / 66
Ever on Sunday / 69
Brunch / 72
Home cooking / 74
Luncheon for one please, James / 77
Playing away / 79
Getting it regular / 82
Dress / 86
Care and training of waiters / 88
Cloth ears / 93
Ugly customers / 94
Smokeism / 97
Why are we waiting? / 99
Troublemaking / 104
The deserving rich / 108
The deserving poor / 111
Fifty uses of lunch / 115
The good mood guide / 117

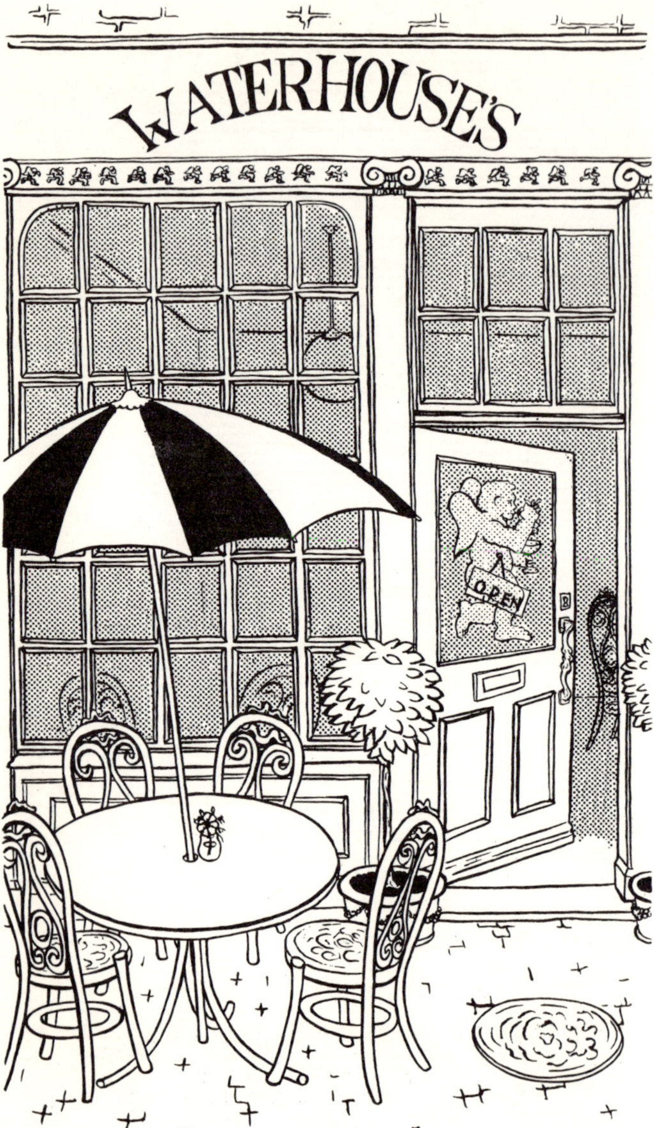
WATERHOUSE'S
OPEN

What This Book Is Not

I KNOW OF only one pleasure of the flesh more acceptable than lunch – and lunch is so perfect a curtain-raiser to it that they make a classic double bill.

But it is exclusively in praise of the supporting attraction that I am here to sing. I had better make it clear from the start that I have not launched on this exercise from any great knowledge of food or love of eating. Food comes into it, of course, as snow comes into ski-ing and water into fishing; but it is the institution of lunch itself, over and above its edible parts, that I find so very agreeable. It is the aim of this little treatise to dissect and analyse lunch as a total experience engaging all the five senses, rather than dwell upon what the wine and leek sauce on the lightly-cooked scallops might have done to give slight offence to the taste-buds.

And so let us establish that this is not a good food guide – or a bad food guide either.

It does not recommend restaurants, though it names a few personal favourites in passing.

It does not pretend to be knowledgeable about wine but it does have something to say about lunchtime drinking, which embraces wine.

It is not concerned with fads or fashions in lunch-eating; nor with asking, much less answering, the question Whither Lunch? Lunch being an absolute, in its perfect state it is incapable of any but the most superficial change or improvement.

It is not about eating out in general nor eating in for that matter. It makes no claim to be an authority on breakfast, elevenses, tea, dinner (but see *Why lunch is not dinner*), supper or bedtime cocoa. My brief is lunch, and lunch only.

Short History of Lunch

THE COMPLETE HISTORY of lunch is that we used not to eat it.

Dinner, taken in mid-afternoon, was the main meal of the day. When, with the idea of giving the toiling masses more time to toil in, dinner began to get pushed further and further into the evening, the need to fill the gap between it and breakfast first arose, and man, alone among the domesticated animals, came to require and expect a midday meal.

Thus lunch was a prime example of that which, if it did not exist, it would be necessary to invent.

True Lunch was pioneered by the upper classes who gave luncheon parties to while away time that had previously been occupied in getting ready for dinner. Although three or four elaborately-prepared courses might be served, its purpose was to amuse — to give the glitterati something to glitter about during the daylight hours. Then restaurants were established to dilute and distort the concept by offering lunch to City clerks and such who, with the decline of the knife-and-fork breakfast and no prospect of supper till seven, were simply looking for something to eat half-way through the day's labours.

Fortunately, not everyone had an office stool to hurry back to. There were enough bohemians on hand with time to spare for a second brandy as to call a host of cheap and cheerful Soho eating-houses into being. Meanwhile, at the top end of the market, the shunting of the idle rich into service flats and their concomitant servant problem created a market for less utilitarian restaurants where they could carry the torch for True Lunch until relieved of the responsibility by the twin

SHORT HISTORY OF LUNCH

innovations of the public relations industry and the expense account.

True Lunch has ever since flourished, despite the ravages of war, austerity, inflation, taxation, redevelopment, refurbishment, inner city blight, mergers and takeovers, health fads, slimming crazes, nouvelle cuisine, fast food, VAT, legislation (President Carter sought to abolish the three-martini lunch: its British equivalent has long been non-deductible for tax purposes), fire regulations, council inspectors, planning laws, staff shortages, customer shortages and Acts of God. Long may it continue to do so.

What Lunch Is Not

It is not what luncheon vouchers are for.

It is not a meal partaken of, however congenial the company, with the principal object of nourishment – eg, two office friends popping over to the friendly little Indian place which everyone uses so much that it's known as the Canteen.

It is not prawn cocktail, steak and Black Forest gâteau with your accountant or bank manager.

It is not, as a rule (but see qualification below), business – particularly if this involves overseas persons you have never clapped eyes on before, and even more particularly if briefcases stuffed with printouts or samples are brought to the table.

It is not literary, civic, commemorative, award presentation, annual office, or funeral.

It is not when either party is on a diet, on the wagon or in a hurry.

Despite Stephen Sondheim's toast to the Ladies Who Lunch, it is not going Dutch.

It is not what Foodies do when they go out in the midday sun.

It is not taken perched on stools at a ledge. Deli food is delicious but it is not lunch.

If taken in a private house, it is not pot luck.

It is not a picnic, though it may by all means, and on occasion even preferably (see *Eating on t' street*) be taken alfresco, if at a properly constituted table.

Lunch at the Club is not lunch. Nor is a luncheon club luncheon.

It is not pub grub. Or wine bar grub – Real Lunch-eaters don't eat quiche.

If involving children, it is not a pizza palace or

WHAT LUNCH IS NOT

hamburger heaven, delightful though all the constituents may be.

It is not a palatable antidote to unpalatable advice, friendly words of warning, 'sounding out' or lobbying.

It is not a duty.

Or a bribe.

Or a penance.

For what lunch is, read on.

[6]

What Lunch Is

*I*F YOU ASK me to nominate my perfect lunch I am spoiled for choice, but upon mature and mouth-watering reflection, and narrowing it down to my most perfect lunch ever, I have to whisk myself back a few summers to the vine-hung terrace of Locanda Cipriani, the famous trattoria on the island of Torcello in the Venetian lagoon.

It takes no effort to recall the simple meal – a delicious light canneloni, a plate of grilled prawns, a salad, wild strawberries – but equally well I can remember, in dazzling detail, the saucer of olives on the table, the little jar of toothpicks, the basket of bread, the oil and vinegar, a bowl of cut lemons. The picture remains so vivid that it is like having been inside a still life. The sun blazed down, but we were deep in scented shadows, and the wine was mountain-stream cool. The *campanile* bell tolled sleepily. A cat basked in the garden (I am very fond of restaurant cats). And Charlie Chaplin sat at the next table. What more could serendipity provide?

That is an illustration of lunch. I will now attempt a definition.

Lunch is a mid-day meal taken at leisure in, usually, a public place (sometimes too public for their liking) by, ideally, two people. Three's a crowd, four always split like a double amoeba into two pairs, six is a meeting, eight is a conference. I make an exception of boisterous family parties, when any number can play.

It is essential that the diners – no, we must not call them diners, and the alternative 'lunchers' would have caught on by now if it were ever going to. Let us settle for 'lunch companions' as the restaurant writers invariably dub their guests whose rather dry *turbot au sauce moutarde* was a less fortunate choice than the pig's trotter stuffed with sweetbreads. The expression may be slightly devalued by now – there is a lot of looking gift horses in the mouth from those ungrateful freeloaders in the restaurant columns – but it defines exactly what lunch is all about: companionship.

It is essential, then, that the lunch companions are drawn together by some motivation beyond the pangs of hunger or the needs of commerce. A little light business may be touched upon, provided always that it is of a congenial nature – I can think of no more agreeable way of having a book commissioned, all publishers being born lunch companions – but it must always be peripheral to the occasion, which is firmly social.

Friendship, of course, is a wide term. Delightful though it always is to see an old chum, it can be even more delightful to become better acquainted with a new one, of the opposite sex. Lovers are great lunch-eaters – so, often, are ex-lovers. Then again: the couple at the corner table may conceivably be husband and wife (though not necessarily one another's) or they may be the most platonic of just good friends. Whatever their status, and whether they know it or not, for as long as they linger in the restaurant they are having an affair. The affair is lunch. How far it may subsequently go (or has previously gone) must not concern us here – though you may be sure it will be a matter for keen conjecture at the other tables of this public boudoir. (Engaging in idle speculation about one's fellow lunch companions is as much an element of lunching out as reading the menu.)

Lunch is a celebration, like Easter after the winter. It is a conspiracy. It is a holiday. It is euphoria made tangible, serendipity given form. Lunch at its lunchiest is the nearest it is possible to get to sheer bliss while remaining vertical.

Why Lunch Is Not Dinner

But, it might be argued, everything I have said so far about lunch may equally be applied to dinner. Not so.

Dinner, however enjoyable, lacks a certain spicy something – that faint but distinct air of foreignness that always hangs over lunch, bringing with it the heady tang of forbidden fruits. There is something ever so slightly wicked about even the most innocent lunch – a feeling of self-indulgence, of stolen moments, of lotus-eating. Even Sunday lunch, over which one is surely entitled to linger after a hard week's work, is accompanied by a pleasurably guilty awareness that one could be more healthily, if not more happily, occupied.

Dine, and you are unwinding after the day's labours. Lunch, and you are playing truant.

Lunch may be mildly – or intensely – illicit ('You do not,' counselled that congenial lunch companion, restaurant critic and man of letters Christopher Matthew, 'take your wife out to lunch'). Dinner, except when indulged in by out-of-town businessmen, rarely so – the affair that has reached the dining-out stage has gone far beyond the flirtatious parameters of lunch and is heading for the divorce courts (The Wig & Pen Club opposite them serves a first-rate lunch. Your lawyer will probably be a member).

You most decidedly do take your wife to dinner – there would be trouble if you did not – together with two other couples you owe a meal to. Reciprocation and obligation hang heavy in the air like garlic. At least one of the party will turn up late and half-cut ('Peter's going to catch up with us at the restaurant as soon as he can get away') and one of the couples will be plainly

THE THEORY & PRACTICE OF LUNCH

suppressing an ongoing domestic row. The bill will be staggering – there are always more guests at dinner than at lunch, they drink more and eat more, and anyway dinner costs more. You will awake with a hangover.

Admittedly, dinner at its best can be a very jolly occasion, but jolliness of that particular order and at that number of decibels is not really a characteristic of lunch, unless it is a special occasion.

The nearest approximation to lunch in the evening is the romantic candlelit dinner for two, where both parties are single and as fancy-free as maybe. But here again there is an important distinction. Dinner, in these circumstances, tends to lead to bed – lunch not necessarily so. You do not (except by long-standing arrangement) as a rule offer to escort a girl home after lunch. Both or either of you may have things to do, offices to go back to, appointments to keep, a birthday card to buy. You have options to keep open or not as you choose, unlike the dinner companion who can hardly claim to be going off to pick up the dry-cleaning at getting on for midnight.

So where dinner is a commitment, lunch retains an elusiveness all its own. It is a shadow play – the delicious hint of a promise, perhaps, but not a pledge.

Lunch, as opposed to dinner, is where you can invite a charming lady without her boring husband, or a fascinating man without his boring wife. Dinner is an obligation or even a retaliation. Lunch is free will.

Useful Phrases

'Listen, why don't we start the proceedings with a nice glass of champagne?'
'You're not in any great hurry to get back, are you?'
'Could my guest have a packet of Benson and Hedges, please?'
'Let's have the other half while we look at the menu.'
'You may have whatever you wish, my love.'
'Could I have my chips on a side plate, please, so that my guest can dip into them?'
'Taste this – it's delicious.'
'Mmmm – yours is good too.'
'Do you think we could manage another bottle?'
'I think we must take this place up.'
'One cheesecake and two forks, please.'
'Not yet, thank you – we'll just stay with the wine.'
'Just coming up to three, actually, but don't worry – they're very relaxed about the licensing laws here.'
'May we have some more coffee, please?'
'I've got some bumph for you somewhere, but I can always shove it in the post.'
'Listen, why don't we conclude the proceedings with a nice glass of champagne?'
'Let me just ring the office and say I've been held up.'
'Good heavens, we seem to be the last ones here.'
'This has been so lovely, we really must do it again soon.'
'How about next Wednesday?'

Ambience

If the food is good, that's great. If the food is great, that's good. But while a bad meal can never make a good lunch, it does not follow that a fantastic meal makes a fantastic lunch, other things not being equal.

The secret is in that over-used word ambience, the quality Michelin gives crossed knives and forks for rather than rosettes. Everything has to be just right: the surroundings, the service, the position of the table, the mix of fellow lunch companions, the lighting, the noise levels.

It is one more element that separates bona fide lunch companions from conventional diners-out. Serious eaters scarcely notice their surroundings. Frivolous eaters always do. Between the rosettes and the crossed knives and forks, a true lunch companion would always opt for the cutlery.

Ambience is to places what charisma or sex appeal is to people: you either have it or you don't. In neither case is it necessary to dress up to the nines for the effect to be made. True, if you have it you should flaunt it, as does the Café Royal Grill – a magnificent painted tart of a room, all plush and gilt and caryatids reflected in the mirrors. Yet equally full of character is Chez Victor in Soho, one of the plainest, most unpretentious-looking restaurants in London – so utilitarian in its old-fashioned way that were it not as steeped in Frenchness as a dish of *escargots* it could be mistaken for an East End cocoa rooms. '*Le patron mange ici*' boasts the little sign that is one of the sights of Soho; it also looks as if *le patron* did the decorating. But the place oozes with atmosphere: you

◯◯ AMBIENCE ◯◯

know as soon as you set foot across the threshold that you are in for a good lunch.

On the other hand, there are restaurants where the designer has been given a blank cheque and they have all the ambience of the fabrics department at Harvey Nichols.

A restaurant's atmosphere has usually grown on it over the years, like the patina of nicotine on the walls and the scuff marks on the banquettes. Instant ambience is difficult to achieve. The room can be pleasing to the eye yet there will be that indefinable something wrong. Are the tables too far apart, is there an echo, is the ceiling too low, are the lights too bright, does the kitchen activity intrude? Or, not so indefinably, does it look empty when it's only half-full? If so, the place simply hasn't taken off.

When all's said and done, it is the inhabitants of a restaurant – the servers and the served – who contribute most to its atmosphere, the decor being merely the backdrop to their performance. The staff, particularly, provide the essential ingredient of bustle. The to-and-froing of the waiters, the trundling around of appetising-looking food trolleys, the seating and ushering out of lunch companions – all this ceaseless activity is part of the show, an important constituent of the rich flavour of lunch, so long as the bustle attracts rather than distracts, and you can hear what the people at the next table are quarrelling about.

Enjoying lunch in the right conditions is like at once watching a play and taking part in one. I was never more conscious of the theatricality of the occasion than on my last visit to La Coupole, the vast brasserie on the Boulevard Montparnasse. Owing to the rain, plus a morbid fear when in foreign parts that if we leave it too late we won't get a table (even in an establishment which could probably feed the whole of Paris at one sitting), my lunch companion and I had our napkins firmly tucked under our chins by 11.30 am, when they were so to speak tuning up – still laying tablecloths, cutting bread, arranging hors d'oeuvres, putting out salt and pepper and toothpicks, and generally preparing for the onslaught.

[14]

AMBIENCE

A *kir* saw us through the overture – waiters taking up their stations, a few early customers trickling in, menus distributed. Then the curtain rose on the great lunch spectacular as an enormous Ziegfield chorus thronged on to that vast stage. The chatter became a hubbub and the hubbub became seething bedlam: it was a Toulouse Lautrec painting come to roaring life. A snaking ballet of waiters and commis weaved constantly in and out of the scene, balancing trays like jugglers, whisking tablecloths away like conjurors. We ate. Then the bedlam gradually diminished to a buzz, and the buzz to a murmur, as the cast dispersed and finally only a few stragglers remained for a last reprise of coffee and brandy. Another matinée over. We left at four, glowing.

Ambience is where you find it: it's a kind of fellow feeling that hits you as you walk through the door. From my very first visits I've had that kind of rapport with L'Epicure, one of the last of the authentic, though upper-bracket Soho restaurants; with L'Escargot, both the downstairs brasserie and the rooms upstairs; with the Groucho Club; and with Langan's Brasserie, which for lunch-as-theatre cannot be surpassed (though the theatricality can, from the host's point of view, sometimes be overdone. I once sought to impress a lady by taking her there: at adjoining tables were Olivier, Joan Plowright, John Mortimer, Maggie Smith, Michael Caine and Albert Finney. For all the notice she took of me I might just as well have left her there and gone to the cinema, returning later to pick up the bill).

Clutter

My long-standing lunch companion Christopher Ward, with whom I have had many a congenial lunch at L'Etoile (where we both so much covet the handsome mahogany mobile cigar cabinet that if it is ever put up for sale we shall have to saw it in half if we are to remain friends) told this story in the American Express magazine *Expression!*, which he edits:

'Some years ago, the late Lord Rothermere took out to lunch a young Fleet Street executive in order to offer him the editorship of the *Daily Mail*.

'Just before the coffee was about to be served, the waiter cleared the table and started to spread a clean cloth over the table. The Viscount was outraged. "Are you suggesting that my guest has made such a mess that we require a new tablecloth?" demanded his Lordship.

' "No, my Lord," replied the terrified waiter.

' "Do you know how much it costs to launder a tablecloth?"

' "No?"

' "Then find out."

'A few minutes later, the cowering waiter returned with the information. "Half a crown, Your Lordship."

' "Good," said Lord Rothermere. "Knock half a crown off the bill and we'll keep the old one." '

Rough justice, you may think, but in my opinion the wretched waiter was lucky his Lordship did not buy up the restaurant and throw him out into the street.

By the coffee stage, tablecloths are *supposed* to look the worse for wear. If the cloth does not look as lived in as Spencer Tracy's face, then the lunch has been a failure. It should bear the honourable scars of battle – wine stains, soup stains, olive oil stains, spilled coffee, cigar

CLUTTER

burns – and be strewn with campaign debris in the way of bread crumbs, spilled salt, wine corks, toothpicks, sugar cubes, chocolate mint wrappers, cigarette packets and what have you. The waiter who obliterates this impressive detritus is as a vandal wrecking the Albert Memorial.

A nice messy table is all part of the fun of lunch. A pristine table may look very nice but it also looks as if the fun hasn't yet started. The table should get progressively more shopsoiled and cluttered as the meal wears on. When you survey the once-snowy expanse in front of you, it should be like looking through a shoebox full of old letters. You should see concrete evidence that you have enjoyed an excellent lunch.

Unfortunately, the average waiter has what I call the whisking instinct ingrained. Whisk! and the oil and vinegar are gone, the moment you have dealt with your salad. Whisk! and your empty wine bottle is removed. Whisk! and the bread disappears. Whisk! and the salt and pepper are gone. Whisk! and every crumb and morsel is brushed away, and it is as if your lunch had never been – except for the bill.

'We'll keep that for the moment, thank you' is a good firm line to take with the waiter when he tries to remove your toys. You can hardly stop him brushing bread crumbs away but neither can he stop you making some more. If he wants something to take away, give him your side plates, and eat your bread from the table as the French do. It tastes all the better for it, and makes a lovely mess.

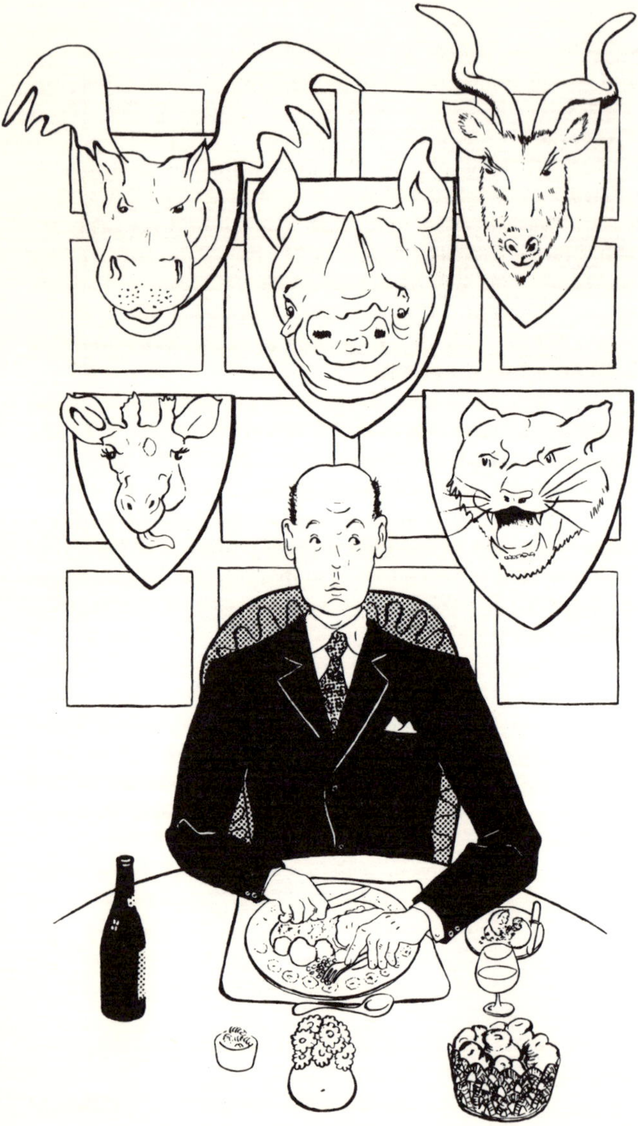

Out Places

THE FOLLOWING MAY be all very well for dinner (or they may very well not be) but they are not suitable for lunch:

Anywhere where you have to ring the doorbell to get in

– or where there is a plywood cut-out of a chef holding a menu by the entrance

– or where, in the glass showcase where the menu ought to be, there is a faded colour photograph of the restaurant, empty

– or where there are two sittings

– or which has a gastronomic menu (except on Sundays, when lunchtime gastronomy is permissible)

– or where the wine list is as thick as the Yellow Pages and adorned with wine labels, maps, and information about grapes

– or where the bill arrives sheathed in a padded leather cover, with a mint

– or which is off the beaten track, unless you know for certain that it does a good lunch trade (nothing is more heartsinking than to arrive at a restaurant which when you went there for dinner was lively and bustling, but which now looks like a culinary Marie Celeste)

– or where the decor features suits of armour, stuffed animals, ships' wheels or the like

– or where the owner is a bit of a character, or they have singing waiters, or go in for jokiness in the slightest degree – ie, bar decorated with currency notes of all nations

– or where there is a snooty notice warning that good food takes time to prepare

– or where coffee and liqueurs are taken in a different room

– or where it is compulsory to sit in the bar until you've ordered, and they don't call you to your table until you've had one dry sherry more than you want, and when you do reach your table the starters are there but the wine is not

– or which allows in itinerant photographers peddling souvenir snapshots

– or where, come three o'clock, the staff stand around with martyred, 'Don't you people have homes to go to?' expressions

– or which has piped music. Or, for that matter, unpiped music

– or which revolves, whether in a clockwise or anti-clockwise direction.

Duties Of The Lunch Companion

Over and above ordinary restaurant good manners – being civil to the waiters, not getting on the nerves of neighbouring tables with loud behaviour (see *Ugly customers*), arriving punctually (fifteen minutes is the maximum margin for latecomers – unlike dinner, lunch cannot always accommodate a late kick-off) and saying thank you when they leave (to the staff, as well as to one another) – lunch companions have certain duties.

The first and most obvious one is towards one another – guest to host as much as host to guest. There must be no division of labour into he/she who entertains and she/he who is entertained. The host, it goes without saying, looks after the guest's every need, whistling up lemons, olive oil, English mustard, ashtrays and so on as well as ordering the wine, making menu suggestions and seeing that everything arrives at the table as it should. But the guest has a duty to respond to these attentions in a suitably appreciative manner, rather than, as many guests do (and particularly women guests, it has to be said) treating the host like a maitre d' (and the maitre d' should not be treated in that disdainful manner, either).

The meal under way and running smoothly, both guest and host are under an obligation to be entertaining – and not only to one another. They are part of the tableau. Which is not to say that they have to make a cabaret act of their conversation, but they should not (married couples are the worst) sit there like dumplings. Lacklustre lunch companions depress everyone around them. They can quarrel if they must – a good lovers' tiff always enlivens lunchtime – but they must not lapse into sulks. Better a dramatic, tearful exit – at least it gives the rest of the room something to talk about.

THE THEORY & PRACTICE OF LUNCH

All other things being equal, lunch companions should disport themselves as if being given a free meal by the management in exchange for sitting in the window attracting new customers by their manifest enjoyment, as used to be the custom of the old New York chop-houses. That is to say, if they're having a good time, then they should not look as if they have just swallowed a fishbone. So many lunch companions remind me of the lugubrious northern audiences the music-hall comedians used to complain about – the ones who'd say 'By the 'eck, you were that funny I had to stop meself from laughing!'

Pleasantries help lunch along. The answer to the maitre d's routine 'Is everything satisfactory?' could be an equally routine 'Everything's fine' or it could be something more enthusiastic. Where justified, a good lunch companion should opt for enthusiasm – they are not going to put it on the bill.

Not only must waiters not be treated like menials, but even menials should not be treated like menials, if only because they're not going to be menials for ever. At the Algonquin in New York of Round Table fame, where I have been lunching three or four times a year for over a quarter of a century, I have always made a point of thanking the bus-boys who clear away plates and fetch glasses of water. One of them I remember from the old days, and who remembers me, is now the head waiter. I always get a table.

Lunch companions should be generous with their praise and not make pernickety complaints about things the waiter can do nothing about. If the soup is cold, send it back. Don't wait for the waiter, upon removing your empty plate, to ask 'How was the soup?' before telling him it was cold. If you leave half your steak because it's tough, by all means say so if asked, or if it's really as tough as old boots, even if not asked. But if you leave it because you just couldn't manage another mouthful it's only polite to murmur a word of apologetic appreciation. Do *not* send your compliments to the chef. If you want to send him anything, send him a bottle.

One of the lunch companion's most important duties

DUTIES OF THE LUNCH COMPANION

– almost a civic responsibility – is to remember where lunch was taken. If the lunch was memorable but the name and address of the restaurant was not, then it is a loss to lunching posterity. This rule particularly applies in foreign parts where friends always need good restaurant recommendations. It is infuriating to be given a rave review of some fabulous bistro where all that is delicious, delightful and delectable can be got for about eight francs including wine, only to be told that the name of it has slipped the endorser's mind but you cross the main square diagonally from the post office, turn down a narrow cobbled street and keep on going until you come to a church when you turn either right or left. The easiest way to make a note of a restaurant's address is to acquire, if it goes in for such fripperies, a bookmatch. I have a huge bowl of restaurant matches, every one a glowing memory, which I discourage guests from putting to practical use. 'That,' I tell them frostily, 'is an extremely good lunch you are lighting your cigarette with.'

Table-hopping

' *I*'M VERY SORRY, sir, but the worst table in the room is reserved – would you like the second worst?'

Thus might the maître d' apologise as he conducts you to the table by the door/the lavatories/the kitchen. Even when they are totally empty, so many restaurants in this country like to use their least attractive tables first, rather than putting their earlybirds in the window to attract custom, as they do across the Channel.

There is no need to accept a badly-positioned table unless the place is packed and the only option is whether to eat there or not. Point boldly at the table you want and say you would like to sit at it. If it is reserved, so be it – grab the next best. But keep a beady eye on the one that is supposedly spoken for, and if it isn't taken, or it is given to a party which quite obviously hasn't booked it, have it out with the maître d'. It may mar your lunch but restaurants really must learn that apart from a few places reserved for regulars, their good tables are not a manorial gift to be bestowed or withheld at whim.

The best plan, if you know the restaurant at all, is to find out the number of the table you fancy and ask for Table No. 9 or whatever when making your reservation. Better still: it is a good idea if the lady lunch companion makes the booking. It will be assumed that she is her consort's secretary; naturally, she will say nothing to disabuse them of the notion but will hint that much depends – business deal, clandestine liaison etc – on getting the table of your choice. Come the actual lunch, they will probably deny all knowledge of your request but be firm.

We're talking about tables you would like to sit at

TABLE HOPPING

because they happen to be nice tables nicely positioned. So-called prestige tables are not worth fighting for. As a matter of fact, little snob value attaches to particular tables in this country, as it does very much in New York, Washington and Los Angeles, where the most fashionable restaurants operate a pecking order, and those in the social swim have been known to walk out because the best table in the house has already been given to Nancy Reagan. (Oddly enough, the New York Lunch Bunch as they are known actually like sitting at the table you and I would turn up our noses at – the one bang next to the door, where being seen compensates for the draught.) Here, the social importance of who sits where seems only to apply in restaurants operating on two floors or in two rooms, when being upstairs or downstairs or in the back room or the front room as the case may be is supposedly the in thing. If you care about such nuances, specify which room you want to be in when you book. More importantly: if downstairs is buzzing and upstairs is empty, don't let them use you as a spearhead to get their upstairs trade moving. Even for two lunch companions who want nothing more than to be alone, an empty restaurant with sounds of conviviality floating up from another room is as depressing as if all the chairs were stacked up and the cleaning lady was mopping the floor.

But to get back to tables. Do you like to sit opposite or side by side? There are two schools of thought. Sitting opposite is good for talking, use of body language – eg, leaning back or forward or turning away – helping one another to forkfuls of food, and playing footsy under the tablecloth. Side by side is good for holding hands, reading the menu together and eliminating 'Don't look now' from the conversational phrase-book in that you can both see everything that is going on, a shared experience which makes lunch a conspiracy.

The snag about sitting opposite is that tables for two are often so small that they might be tables for one. The snag about side by side is that usually the only way to be accommodated thus is at a table for four. Given some

THE THEORY & PRACTICE OF LUNCH

restaurants' reluctance to make their customers comfortable, this can lead to some ridiculous exchanges:

'No, we'd like to sit at that table there, please.'

'Very sorry, but that's a table for four.'

'Yes, but as you're not very busy, we'd like to sit at it.'

'Very well, but you won't mind sharing if another couple come in when there are no more tables.'

'In fact we'd mind very much. Where would you put them if we'd stayed at our table for two?'

'At this table here, I suppose, if there were no others available.'

'This table for four?'

'Yes.'

'Well, then, if you're holding the table for a couple, you need wait no longer.'

In such circumstances, the thing to do is move in on the table of your choice even as negotiations continue, and firmly sit down. The time that managers or head waiters have for argufying is very limited, and as they can hardly throw you out into the street they will capitulate with a shrug and cause the two spare places to be cleared with a resigned air of 'We have a right pair here.' Having won, a little ingratiation will do no harm. Order a good wine and leave a good tip, and in future your insistence on sitting side by side at a table for four will be treated as the harmless foible of a pair of amiable eccentrics, even though it puts them (this is why they didn't want you to have it in the first place) to the enormous trouble of removing two superfluous napkins, sets of cutlery and glasses from the table.

And my final word on tables. As articles of furniture they have been around at least since the days of ancient Greece (when Plato was probably told that the table next to the fountain was reserved for Mr Socrates). When are they going to develop one that doesn't wobble?

The Menu

I wish now that I had stolen one of the menus from sorely-missed Bertorelli's before they stacked up the chairs for the last time in their Charlotte Street premises, a time-warp of a room that whisked you back to the Soho of around 1910. And not only the decor: the menu cover itself, a black and white art nouveau-ish concoction featuring one of those ladies who are all swirls from head to foot, was the original one: and if you slid your purple-smudged, near-indecipherable hand-written menu out of its plastic envelope, you would find underneath the original bill of fare, with sardines in oil at twopence and veal cutlets at ninepence and wines at around one and six a bottle. It was so fascinating that when I took a twelve-year-old to Bertorelli's he thought the item 'cover charge' was for the privilege of poring over that old closely-printed menu while waiting for one's spaghetti bolognese. As well it might have been, and cheap at the price.

Browsing over the menu with an aperitif is, or should be, one of the delights of lunch. To this end, it should be easily readable – legible if hand-written, and not dark brown on light brown or silver on deep red if printed; and the light should not be so dim that you have to hold the menu card over your candle in a bottle and risk setting it on fire.

Giving the menu only a cursory glance because one happens to know it by heart is not on: it is almost as bad as skipping a starter because one isn't really hungry. Even if two lunch companions know perfectly well what they will be having, since that's what they always have at this particular place, a certain amount of dithering over the possible alternatives can only add savour to the meal.

The menu says a good deal about the restaurant and

∽ THE THEORY & PRACTICE OF LUNCH ∾

its pretensions. If it is bound in simulated pigskin like a non-aggression treaty between two very minor nations, its pretentions will be pretentious. If it is the size of a bedsheet with everything available, prepare yourself for a boil-in-the-bag job. If it consists of only five items including the date, then resign yourself to something stuffed and sauced to within an inch of its life, and a chef-owner who will drive you frantic with his 'little touches.' If it is scrawled on a blackboard (to the distraction of short-sighted lunch companions such as myself), it is going to be noisy and cheerful, though perhaps efficiency may not be its strong point.

There is nothing wrong with a long menu if the prices are marked in daily against such dishes as they have been able to market for – the usual arrangement in seafood restaurants (the menu in the cavernous Oyster Bar under New York's Grand Central Station, a mouth-watering catalogue of dabs and chowders and Blue Point oysters and clams and Hangtown Fry and red snapper and Boston scrod and swordfish, reads like a Hemingway short story with the dialogue filleted). There is nothing wrong with a short one either if they will agree to a simple grilled sole without the crayfish sauce it comes with. The ideal menu is of middling length with a reasonable choice of dishes ranging from the plain to the fancy, augmented by a few daily specials which should be written in by hand, as should the fresh vegetables of the day. It should not be over-descriptive – 'Medallion of milk-fed lamb served with its juices scented with basil from Mrs Potter's kitchen garden'; the waiter should know enough about the menu to be able to explain each dish, and to steer lunch companions tactfully away from, eg, ordering starter and main course that come with similar sauces.

The waiter's recitative, indeed, is all part of the show for many people, though personally I draw the line at the maître d' reciting the day's specials at inordinate length, obliging one to go through a glassy-eyed repertoire of sage nods, raised eyebrows, *moues* of appreciation, smiles and grimaces, as if enduring a favourite nephew's

THE MENU

rendering of 'The Wreck Of The Hesperus.' I draw an even firmer line at those elocutionary establishments where with a sinking heart you realise that the entire menu is going to be recited by the waiter, and that as you fix him with the self-consciously attentive expression of a juror listening to the summing-up in a complicated case of financial fraud, you are not going to take in a word he is saying. You come across these places particularly in the middle west of America, where at least it has to be said that the college-girl waitresses, as they usually are, are impressively word-perfect. (I do, however, continue to hope that one of them will depart from the script one day – 'Hi, I'm Abbie Lou and today we have shrimp Louie, a Caesar salad with our very own house dressing and I'm deeply unhappy. Cindy Anne right over there serving the two orders of hamburger platter has stolen my boy friend and that comes with a baked Idaho potato or french fries . . .') I have also heard of a New York restaurant where the waiters arrange themselves around the table in barber shop formation and actually sing the menu, but I have never personally set foot in it nor indeed in the block where it is situated.

For myself, I like a menu that not only provides the right amount of well presented reading matter but which has the wine list built in, so that I can order everything at one go and get the waiter cracking on fetching the wine before he organises the food. Where the wine list comes separately, as it usually does, its dimensions and appearance are a far less infallible guide to the quality of its contents than the menu proper. You can get a wine list like the opening number of a part-work encyclopedia of wine bound in Skivertex, yet its lush undergrowth of hype might conceal an impressive range of reasonably-priced wines intelligently chosen. Or not. Or it may, like Chez Victor's, consist simply of a few lines typed on a rather grubby postcard, and that too could turn out (as it does) a well-selected list. Or not.

Why does the guest get a menu to look at but not a wine list? Convention has it that the choice of wine is with the host, as if he were entertaining in his home; but

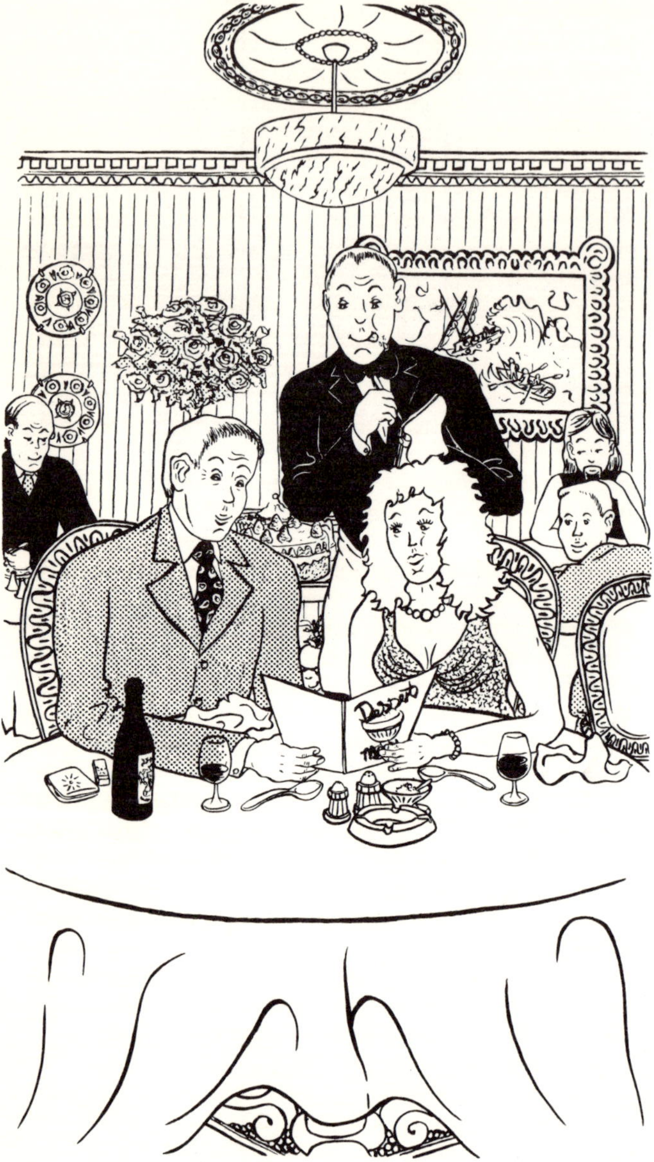

⌒ THE MENU ⌒

in that case why doesn't the choice of food rest with him too? As things stand, it is left to the host to read out the entertaining bits – 'Bloody hell, Château La Mission-Haut-Brion, a hundred and twenty-five quid!' So why can't both share in the fun? I only ask. If it's because it's not considered decent for the guest to know the price of the wine brought to the table, the guest's copy of the wine list could be devoid of prices as the menu sometimes is. Then she could ask for the Château La Mission-Haut-Brion.

If, despite my homily on the subject (see *Only if you will*) you decide to eschew the pudding, do not wave away the dessert menu should this come separately from the main one. Individual dessert menus always make lip-smacking reading. Besides, it could make you change your mind.

And a word about foreign menus. Most of us, however unbilingual we are, can stagger through a French menu. I can order *café*, *caffe* or *Kaffee* in five languages (though without necessarily remembering its sex) and snap my fingers in eight. I know that there are more words for prawn in Italian than I have had hot *colazione*. I even know the Portugese for *Obergruppenführer*, which is 'Psst!' But there are still occasions when the menu is all Greek to me, particularly in Greece, or Double Dutch, as is often the case when I try to get second helpings in Holland.

Dictionaries and phrasebooks are next to useless. I use an invaluable little volume called the *Instant Menu Translator*, published by Foulsham. It's saved me a lot of aggravation at lunch. Say I fancy a light meal of (according to regional variation) *martedi*, *martes* or *mardi*, or *Dienstag* as some German menus call this interesting delicacy, I simply turn up the relevant initial under the relevant language to discover, by the absence of any such dish, that I was on the verge of ordering Tuesday.

The Eating Part

SINCE EATING IS superficially the object of the exercise, we had better have a word or two about it.

The first thing to be said is that lunch should be a whole lunch, not two-thirds of one. Kingsley Amis has rightly identified the most heart-sinking phrase ever encountered in a restaurant as 'Shall we go straight in?' (though it's quite in order if the idea is to get snugly settled in and order drinks at the table. And come to think of it, there are restaurant bars and restaurant bars. The bar as mahogany-panelled, backlit Purgatory, where it is necessary to perch on penitent stools nibbling through a bowl of peanuts in order to expiate the mortal sin of wanting to go in to lunch, is not my idea of a good start). Almost as depressing is 'Just coffee for me, please,' with its prissy implication that all good things must come to an end. So they must, but not before the pud. (Or cheese. Or both.) As for 'I don't think I'll bother with a starter, what about you?', the only thing to be done with a such a bad lunch companion is to order the soup and dunk his head in it. (See *Bad companions*.)

But it is neither necessary nor desirable for a three-course or even four-course lunch to lie like a brick on the stomach. Lay off the steak and kidney pie. Avoid the restaurant famed for its 'ample portions' and go for light dishes and little of them. A lot of places these days, like Langan's Bar & Grill, will let you have a starter as a main course. Some, indeed, make a point of indicating a supplementary charge for starters as main courses, though why there should be a penalty clause for the customer ordering what the customer wants is beyond me. Be that as it may, two starters, a salad and a light pudding with perhaps a bit of Brie will go down very

⳽ THE EATING PART ⳽

well and leave you an appetite for dinner. Keep control of what you're getting – refuse the 'selection of vegetables' – genteelspeak for 'all the trimmings' – and order the vegetable or vegetables you want. Conversely, if you want more of anything, there's no reason why you shouldn't ask for it. I wonder why no-one ever dreams of asking for a second helping of salad?

Simple food makes the best lunch. I don't mean simple to the point of half-wittedness but free of rich sauces and not rolled up in a pastry casing and stuffed with apricots. In other words, not cordon bleah. I have no rooted objection to pretty patterns of kiwi fruit or kaleidoscopic arrangements of thinly sliced carrot. Nouvelle cuisine is suffering from a meat-two-veg-and-dumplings backlash these days, but gone about properly, as at L'Escargot for example, it adds just the right touch of fussed-about-withness to make the dish look interesting and give it that extra pinch of flavour. And, important to many lunch companions, the helpings are such that you don't need to ask for a doggy bag.

I would far rather have too little on my plate than too much. To someone of small appetite, nothing is so off-putting as a heap of food that would sustain Mother Hubbard and her brood for a week. It is all the worse when you are in a restaurant where you know the maître d' is going to be persistent in asking if something is wrong if you don't eat up. Let him enquire if the meal was to your satisfaction, by all means, but not make you feel as if you were back eating school dinners and couldn't manage your tapioca. (I secretly approve of those American restaurants which, having given you enough steak to feed Texas, take not the smallest interest in whether you eat it or not.) It is also daunting when the starter is enormous – you immediately start wondering how you are ever going to get through your main course, and why on earth you ordered what will plainly turn out to be your own weight in vegetables. In Italy, restaurants will often serve the first course before enquiring what you would like for the second, and very sensible too, since how you view the prospect of the *osso bucco* before you have had your *spaghetti carbonara* might not tally with how you view it afterwards. I appreciate that following that custom here would present enormous problems for the kitchen, but not following it can sometimes present enormous problems for the gastric system.

For preference, I nearly always lunch off fish, chicken or liver. Give me the Neal Street's avocado and bacon salad, a grilled sole and a sorbet, or Langan's fish soup, charcoal grilled liver with onions, and the strawberry tart, and I will sign an affidavit that God's in his heaven and all's right with the world. But the meal, for me, is not a meal in itself. It has to be supported by all manner of little extras – crudités and olives to toy with, bread to crumble and mop up juices with, dark chocolates to nibble, and plenty of coffee.

A sign of a good lunch – having just eaten one, that is – is if you still maintain a lively curiosity in what is being conveyed to the other tables. If what you have had has satisfied your appetite, but not dulled it, then a good job has been done by all.

Watching other people eating should be one of the side-delights of lunch. It need not be, in fact it would not be a pleasure if it were, in a spirit of envy or gluttony. I do not, myself, care for *moules marinière* or *fruits de mer* but I love to see them being tucked into, particularly from those great dustbin lids that you see more on continental tables than on our own.

I am also a great pudding watcher. I once stayed at a place in Cap Ferrat where the speciality of the house was pudding. When, of a Sunday lunchtime, the chef wheeled out his latest creations, the whole restaurant was agog, like children with their noses pressed to the sweetshop window; and everyone took the keenest interest in what everyone else was having. This lip-smacking prurience was sustained on Monday, though now tinged with anxiety in case the confection we would have plumped for yesterday had we not been too tempted by something else, had. already been guzzled. The mouth-watering would have subsided by Tuesday when the remains of Sunday's sweets had begun to take on the

THE EATING PART

appearance of Mrs Pooter's oft-presented blancmange, and the chef no longer deigned to appear in person but sent out his deputy. But on Wednesday the whole rigmarole started again and once more we were like orphans given a Christmas party. Taking an interest in someone else's chocolate roulade or hazelnut mousse is so much one of the vicarious pleasures of life that I am only surprised one cannot be arrested for it.

Which brings me to looking at the food in general. Pondering over the hors d'oeuvre trolley and subsequently the cheeseboard and sweet trolley, not to mention monitoring what's coming out of the kitchen while you consider the menu, is as much an integral part of the lunch experience as the eating. By priming the gastric juices so, you are getting far more out of your lunch than you are paying for, at least as regards the actual intake of groceries.

You should not leave the lunch table feeling that you do not want any dinner. You should leave the lunch table feeling that you would like to have lunch all over again. And since both of you have your Filofaxes about you, what's to stop you arranging it there and then?

Lemons

If there is any single item of produce to be found in the kitchen that quintessentialises the ideal restaurant, it is the lemon.

Lemons bring the Mediterranean to the table. The absence of lemons brings a touch of the Irish Sea.

In any restaurant new to me, I regard their attitude to lemons as the acid test, or citrus test rather, of whether I am likely to get a decent lunch.

Considering that a lemon costs only about the price of a couple of bread rolls, it is remarkable how mean some places can be with this essential ingredient of their calling. You would think there was still a war on, when a banana was an event and a lemon a miracle.

It starts at the bar when they ask if you want ice and lemon in your gin and tonic (or worse, they don't ask, so you have to remind them). Asking if you want ice and lemon in your gin and tonic is like asking if you want pepper and salt with your meal, but in the mean-minded joint you have stumbled into they would not care, as a voluntary act, to be seen producing anything more than the absolute minimum they can get away with without prosecution under the Weights and Measures Act. The lemon, when it is produced, is a transparent sliver riddled with pips and the ice consists of one half-melted cube. You know already, or by now should be able to divine, that the place serves portion-controlled melon. The point is that if the restaurant is mean with its lemons it is going to be mean with everything. It is going to have a mean manager who will employ mean staff, who will regard it as their role to give the customers a mean time.

Do not order the fish. It will arrive garnished with a wafer-thin half slice of lemon dunked in parsley. Call for

LEMONS

lemon to squeeze over your sole and you will be brought, if they ever get round to it and after you have been made to feel like Oliver asking for more, a supplementary wafer minus the parsley, but with no instructions on how it is supposed to be squeezed.

If they do run to a whole wedge of lemon, it will probably come shrouded in muslin – I suspect so you cannot tell it has already been slightly used or will be used again, like the teabags.

I won't lunch, or anyway I won't lunch a second time, in any restaurant where they do not throw lemons about as if they grew on trees. Scurvy victims were given lemons – why can't I be? When I order lemon I require it to be understood that I am speaking in the plural. At the very least I want three or four generous wedges in a saucer. Better, a whole lemon quartered or halved, with a standing offer of reinforcements if needed. Best of all, in that rare establishment where it is comprehended that lemons do furnish a restaurant, an entire bowl of lemons, some to squeeze and the rest to look at, and to smell.

A Glass Of Water

LOOKING FOR FILM locations in the north, the extremely urbane, Italian-born producer Jo Janni allowed Willis Hall and me to conduct him into a modest café in Halifax for a wholesome lunch of plate-sized Yorkshire puddings, a cut off the joint and two veg. The place being unlicensed, Jo asked for a glass of water.

The previous evening, in a humble fish-and-chip shop boasting two oilcloth-covered tables for la-di-da customers who wished to partake of their supper with a knife and fork instead of on the hoof out of newspaper, he had requested – and got – a simple green salad dressed with oil, vinegar and a little mustard.

Water, however, was something else again. 'What's up?' the motherly waitress asked Willis in a loud stage whisper. 'Has he got to take some tablets?'

Asking for a glass of water, I've often found, is a good test of a restaurant's efficiency and attention to detail. Tap water, that is – designer water will arrive as promptly as anything else that is going on the bill, and with ice and lemon, and in a nice glass.

It's amazing what a hash some reputable restaurants can make of serving a plain glass of water. In the first place, you probably have to ask for it three or four times, no-one backstage being programmed to handle so simple a request. (Hotel dining room staff, for some reason, are particularly inept at finding a cold tap and turning it anti-clockwise.)

Then, when it does arrive, it can look so unattractive and tepid that you really would think it was meant to wash down 'some tablets.' Yet simply by being served with lots of ice, in a glass that doesn't look as though it had been picked up from the Oxfam shop (I have had

A GLASS OF WATER

water banged down in front of me in a *brown* glass, which made it look like mud) plain water can look as appetising as any other dish on the table.

Gravetye Manor near East Grinstead, where I have occasionally enjoyed as elegant a Sunday lunch as it is possible to find, put bottles of their own spring water on the table, and very refreshing it is too. Not every restaurant has access to an artesian well but what's wrong with a jug?

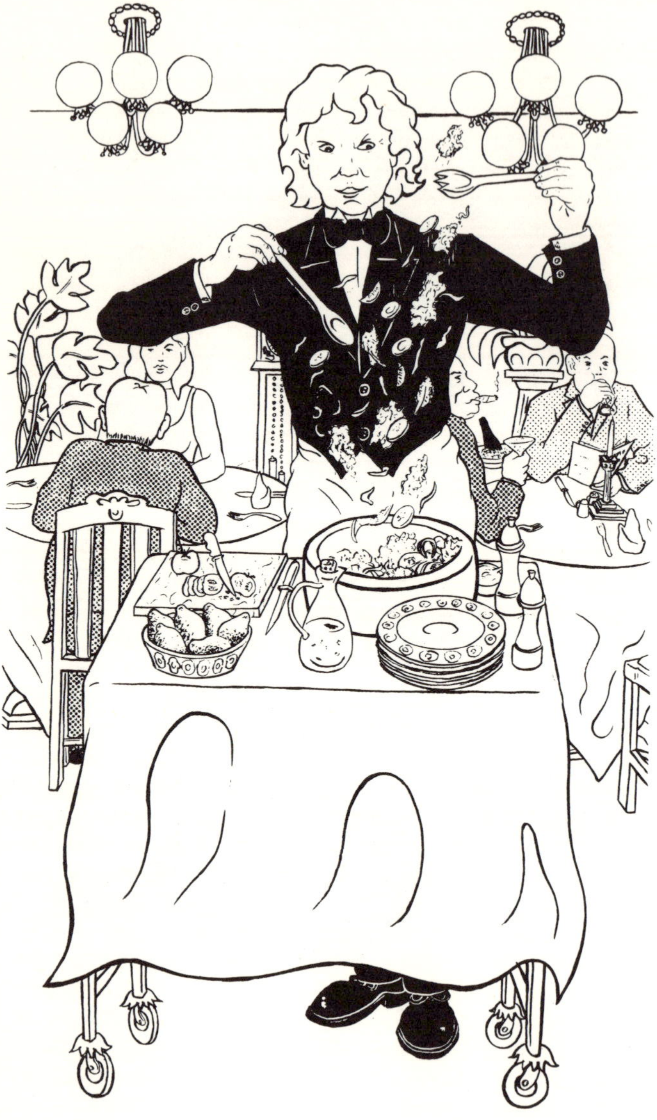

A Nice Salad

When Aneurin Bevan said that this island was made of coal and surrounded by fish, of which only a genius could arrange a shortage at the same time, he might have added that its topsoil is covered in succulent, edible greenery, which only a cretin could convert into an indifferent salad.

A nice side salad being an essential ingredient of lunch, it is a pity that so many places do not know how to serve one.

Everyone has their own idea of the perfect salad. Mine consists of a thinly-sliced tomato with oil and lemon, nothing else. It is remarkably difficult to come by. Either it arrives garnished with parsley, or worse, chopped onions, or the waiter has simply not listened (see *Cloth ears*) and comes back with a mixed salad in which wedges of tomato predominate.

I like the oil and lemon to be put on the table so that I can prepare the dressing as I wish, which means having enough of it swimming about on the plate for me to dunk my bread in when the salad is eaten. The staff may be the bee's knees at mixing oil and lemon, but fetching a salad to the table pre-dressed is only one up from the workman's caff practice of serving the cuppa already sugared.

Failing my simple tomato, I can happily fall in with the waiter who wheels across a portable kitchen and proceeds to make a production number of my salad with a big wooden bowl and all the works. This is all part of the agreeable kitschness of one style of lunch, and the exercise does usually produce a good, well-dressed salad, with the customer getting a say in the ingredients.

I do not care for ready-made salads which are nearly

always disfigured by something I don't want, notably cubed beetroot, cucumber or/and spring onions – elements which give the impression that if only the kitchen staff had known where to get their hands on tinned salad, they would have served it.

I like my salad arranged on a plate, not crammed into a dish – and particularly not one of those kidney-shaped dishes that look like accessories to a gallstone operation.

For those who like to toy with their food at lunchtime, as many of us do regardless of reproachful nannyish glances at our not eating up our greens, a good salad makes an excellent starter. You can pick at it while your more peckish companion is downing oysters, then keep the remains as a side salad with the main course – provided they don't whisk your plate away while you're not looking, or even when you are. At one trattoria staffed by obsessive clearers-away I logged no fewer than six separate attempts to wrest my salad plate from me. Finally conceding defeat, they sulkily refused to have anything more to do with it, and it was still on the table when I left.

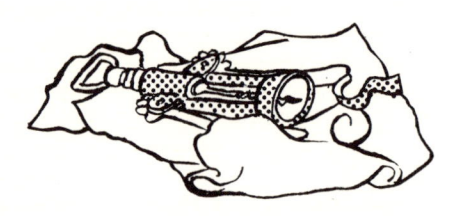

Only If You Will

There was a time in living memory when the squeak across terrazza-tiled floor of pudding trolley laden with profiteroles and caramelised oranges had every lunch companion's mouth watering. You were expected to indulge in a sweet and indulge in a sweet you did. These days, discounting the steakhouse circuit where the surf 'n' turf set tuck into portion-controlled Black Forest gâteau and jam-smeared cheesecake like Henry I at the lampreys, the word seems to be going about that Real Men Don't Eat Pud, and that real women won't eat pud because they're on the Oxford/Cambridge/Luton Polytechnic Diet.

Real women, unreal women also, will eat pud – at least occasionally for a treat even if they're slimming – but they have to be coaxed.

Asked if she would like a sweet, the typical female lunch companion, after humming and hawing and casting covetous glances at the gooey strawberry tartlets, will probably concede at last, 'Only if you're having one too.' Typical male lunch companion, however, probably nursing a dark suspicion that any pudding that's not hot apple pie or jam roly-poly is effeminate, will decline – or at best volunteer, 'No, but I'll tell you what, I'll have some cheese.' Whereupon female lunch companion will say, 'Oh, then I shall have cheese as well' and the moment is lost.

Not that I have anything at all against cheese – indeed, some of my most memorable lunches have ended with cheese, though I wish they would stop offering me biscuits with it and just leave the basket of bread on the table where it was doing no harm – but it is a pity. If you were to toss up a coin between cheese and pud –

tossing between either cheese or pud and just coffee would be no contest – then the sweet course has to win heads down. That's to say, if the lunch companions are of opposite sexes. Let me put it this way: you never hear of a couple ordering one piece of cheese and two knives.

But you do hear them ordering one slice of cheesecake and two spoons. Sharing a pud or swopping spoonfuls – gooseberry fool, like grass, is always greener on the other side of the fence – is one of the pleasurable little observations of true lunch companionship. Sweet-sharing at the lunch table clicks up a happy snapshot, something to remember, and that forms a bond. The couple who scoff *crème brûlée* together, stay together.

Furthermore a silly, prettily-presented little sweet course – the kind of frothy confection you may expect to find briefly listed in monastic calligraphy at such places as craftily tempt you with a separate and altogether enticing dessert menu like the renowned Box Tree at Ilkley (though if the Box Tree tempts you to lunch it will have to be at eight in the evening) – can only add to the wickedness of the lunch sensation, that abandoned, defiantly anti-puritan feeling that you are engaging in an act that was probably illegal until about 1951.

And you can always have the cheese afterwards. Or before. But please, not instead of.

Even so, I refuse to eat any sweet off any menu where the choice is headed 'Your Just Desserts,' or which features Mrs Butterfield's Rhubarb Crumble or whatever. The experience should have overtones of the bedroom, not the nursery.

The Drinking Part

A FURTHER VARIATION on K. Amis's 'Shall we go straight in?' heartstopper is 'Shall we go straight on to wine?' No, we shall not, we shall have an aperitif, and the waiter will preferably be at the table asking 'Would you like something from the bar?' before our bums have touched the seats.

My own favourite opener is a vodka martini, if it's so well constructed that it leaves me stirred not shaken. Joe Allen's serves a perfect one, as is only to be expected: but it is surprising how many otherwise spot-on places serve a lukewarm, ill-proportioned imperfect one, considering that cocktails are now as common as Coca-Cola along the King's and Fulham Roads. Italians cannot produce a good vodka martini, and neither can anyone who calls it a vodkatini.

A properly-prepared Bloody Mary, with 'all the works' as barmen are fond of designating their arsenal of Tabasco etc, is alternatively a perfect curtain-raiser to lunch. A strong Bloody Mary, in the course of blowing one's head off, clears the sinuses, activates the palate and generally tones up the system, thus fostering the complacent delusion that you are taking something breakfastly wholesome like bran flakes.

Otherwise, what you will, with tonic or soda and chinking with ice – provided that what you would is not another and another and another. One aperitif – oh, very well then, two – should be enough, provided that the meal has been ordered and the wine is on the table by the time you've drained your glass. (If it hasn't and it isn't and it's not your fault, you should be lunching somewhere else.) Three, and you're feeling sticky round the lips and have taken the edge off your appetite. Four,

THE THEORY & PRACTICE OF LUNCH

and lunch becomes a mere appendage to a drinking session.

Now to the wine.

Good wine, not plonk. The house wine by all means, if it is well-selected (a tinge of wine snobbery still hovers in this area, some uncertain souls believing their guests, and worse, the waiter, will think them cheapskate if they settle for house wine). And for preference, something crisp, white and light rather than something red and fruity that tastes as if it is good for the blood.

Guy Deghy, my co-author on a history of the Café Royal years ago, asks rhetorically: 'What were the Café Royal wits witty on? Not the heavy red burgundies but yellow wine and Seltzer.' It is perfectly true, though how George Bernard Shaw sparkled on Apollinaris I don't know. Perhaps, like most of those lunch-hour teetotallers who have a heavy workload on 'so I'll stick to Perrier if it's all the same to you,' he didn't. But there's no doubt that the wine that travels best with the lunchtime banter and gossip is not served at room temperature.

However, if your guest wants claret then claret your guest must have, even if you have to re-think your lunch choice to go with it. I am hotly anti the one-half-bottle-of-each policy, whereby guest and host get what they each want to drink independently. It is anti-social: part of the companionship of being lunch companions is that you should take your wine from the same bottle. It is, to be fanciful, as symbolic as breaking bread.

Besides, by some miraculous process which is the reverse of the loaves and fishes, whereas a whole bottle may be just enough for the two of you, half a bottle is never quite enough for just one of you. As a matter of fact, if you keep the kind of company I myself am fortunate enough to lunch with, a whole bottle itself is never enough (half bottles are unheard of), which is another reason for sticking to dry white instead of calling up a second bottle of Côte de Beaune and an hour later falling asleep at one's desk.

The one hazard in ordering white wine is that the waiter may take it into his head to place the bottle out

THE DRINKING PART

of arm's reach, like the grapes of Tantalus in an ice bucket. I like to be in total control of my wine-flow and always insist on the wine being on the table, thus eliminating the lunch-spoiling agitation factor (see *Indigestifs*) of having to catch the waiter's eye when I want the glasses re-filled, which is always at a faster rate than he would seem to deem necessary. If the wine is properly chilled then it doesn't need to stand in an ice bucket at the other side of the room; if it does need an ice bucket then it should go back. (You still do not have to look very far in this country to find house white wine and particularly house champagne unchilled, the thinking presumably being that there is no call for it.)

But getting back to that second bottle: the truth is that the ubiquitous 70 cl bottle is too small for your average pair of lunch companions, a fact which is always recognised by any party of three who will invariably order two bottles to arrive at once, thus upping their ration from the standard rate for couples of half a bottle each to the standard rate for threesomes of a considerably more acceptable two-thirds. A litre bottle is about right for two people, but unless you are in an Italian place where they do those seemingly bottomless flasks of Chianti, a litre bottle is hard to come by. So, infuriatingly, is a half-bottle of whatever it is you have been drinking. And so you either settle for two bottles or you top up on a glass of house wine – an acceptable compromise, that, since having had one glass you can always have another. Or, if you're going to make a song and dance about having cheese, you could switch to half a bottle of a nice warm red.

An even more acceptable compromise, for my taste, is half a bottle of champagne, particularly (see *Only if you will*) if indulging in pudding. Champagne, indeed, in the right weather and in the right setting and with something to be euphoric about – Midsummer's Day at the Mirabelle, say, in celebration of being able to afford it – can make a delightful accompaniment to the entire meal. The justly-celebrated Geale's in Notting Hill, which serves the best fish and chips south of Leeds, does a roaring

‿✐ THE THEORY & PRACTICE OF LUNCH ‿✐

trade in fish and chips and champagne. You only need to try it once to see champagne forever after as essential a condiment as salt and vinegar. And champagne goes with bacon and eggs at Kettner's in Romilly Street like – well, like eggs and bacon.

'Liqueurs, port or brandy and cigars, sir?' Outside the office Christmas lunch, this street cry of old London as the sommelier wheels over his pedlar's trolley of bottles and boxes seems to be meeting with an evermore negative response. Cigar-smoking particularly is on the wane since the habit was declared anti-social (see *Smokeism*). Brandy, like pud, now falls into the 'Only if you will' class where a good deal of conscience-wrestling has to be seen to be gone through before temptation is yielded to and large ones ordered. As for me, I no longer smoke and these days I find brandy a little drowse-inducing, but I like to see my fellow lunch companions enjoying their brandy and cigars, just as I like to see them devouring oysters for all that oysters and I are no longer on speaking terms. Yet the brandy fumes and the wisp of cigar smoke induce a slight touch of melancholy at the realisation, as coffee cups are drained, that the show is now over. There is no going back on a large Hine VSOP and a fat cigar. Personally I like to keep the feast a little more open-ended. Have another glass of champagne and change your mind about the strawberries Romanov.

A further difference between lunch and dinner, incidentally, is that it is Not Done to arrive for lunch drunk. How one leaves is another matter.

Bad Companions

'*J*UST PERRIER.'

'You won't mind if I dash off at two – I've got someone coming into the office.'

'Shall we get the ordering out of the way and then we can get down to business?'

'Oh, I'll just have an omelette or something – I don't usually each lunch.'

'Are you bothered about wine?'

'By the way, just so we don't get off on the wrong foot, you know I'm living with Simon, don't you?'

'Right, well I suppose you're wondering what this is all about.'

'God, this place has gone downhill, don't you agree?'

'I really don't know why I didn't cancel – I've got a mountain of work on.'

'All right, so long as you don't mind drinking most of it yourself.'

'Should one of us be taking notes, do you think?'

'I was hoping this was going to be a social lunch but I hadn't realised how close we were to the end of the tax year.'

'No, truly – I'll watch you eat yours.'

'I used to come here a lot till I had that bad bout of food poisoning.'

'Would you think me awfully rude if I went over and said hello to Sue for a few minutes – I haven't seen her for yonks?'

'Would you like to take a quick glance at this draft report?'

'You seem tense.'

'No, honestly – that was very filling.'

'You're not looking awfully well – shall I get the bill?'

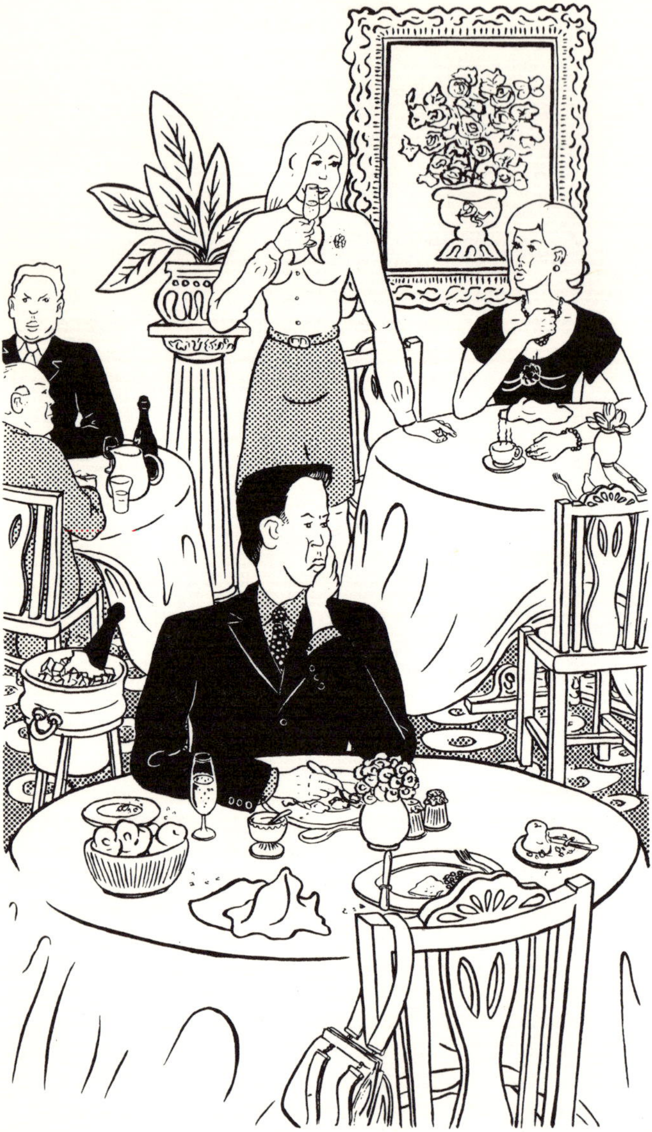

BAD COMPANIONS

'Only if they do decaff.'
'Are you *really* having something from the trolley – I don't know where you put it all.'
'Why don't we split the bill?'
'Have I told you about my operation?'
'Look – I'll come straight to the point, I've got a bit of a cashflow problem.'
'I'm pregnant.'

The Bill

There are really only three things to be said about the bill – that it should be presented promptly when requested, that it should be reasonably legible, and that the total shouldn't include the date.

Non-arrival of the bill at the first time of asking is even more infuriating than its being plonked on the table before it is wanted. (My response to this form of over-zealousness is at once to order two more glasses of wine, necessitating the bill to be taken away and made out again.)

What a shame it is when a restaurant serves a delightful lunch only to bring on a bout of heartburn by refusing to allow the customer to pay for it and leave. My experience is that if the bill isn't produced within a few minutes of being first asked for, it still won't be produced when asked for a second and third time, in which case the only thing to do is get up and head for the door. A screen cowboy trying to leave a western saloon without paying for his fifth of bourbon would stand more chance of making it – restaurant staff hitherto unable to see a plaintively waving arm have eyes in the back of their heads when it comes to spotting a possible defector. But the point is made, and the bill is settled from a standing position in the middle of the room, at no small inconvenience to passing waiters and serve them right.

Some waiters get tetchy when repeatedly asked for the bill – the only-got-one-pair-of-hands syndrome. They might as well protest that they're too busy to fetch the soup or open the wine. Fetching the bill is as important a task for the waiter as any other (indeed, the owner might argue that it is *the* most important). The delay may not be his fault – the accounting bureaucracy of some

THE BILL

restaurants is unbelievable – but in this as in everything else that might go wrong, the waiter is in the position of the royal messenger who gets it in the neck for delivering bad news. Tough, but as they say in the army when the shrapnel's flying, if you can't take a joke you shouldn't have joined.

The bill itself, when it arrives, can bring a sour note to the end of lunch. The worst kind is the computerised one in well-nigh indecipherable mauve ink, with numbers or symbols of bottles and coffee cups to identify the items listed. Like most hotel bills these days, it repeats each figure about half a dozen times before adding it to the running total, thus making it impossible for anyone but an accountant to check it.

Next, in reverse order of incomprehensibility, comes the pre-printed bill where the prices simply have to be entered against the relevant dishes. The figures are usually scrawled in any old order so that it reads 'Couvert 9.35, antipasto 90, zuppa 85, caffe 6.40, vini 1.30' and so on. Then we have the familiar dyslexic bill: 'Crv 1.00, 1 min w p 4.50, 1 mb du 3.95 . . .' And so on down to the curiosity I once came by in a bistro in Notting Hill and thought of framing – a bill that listed what I'd had in clear, rounded handwriting, with prices that matched those on the menu.

While it may not be true that there is no such thing as a free lunch – I have eaten many, and in my turn provided many – there is certainly no such thing as a cut-price lunch, and you expect to pay for what you have had. That doesn't mean to say the customer is not entitled to a clear, legible account of expenses incurred, the same as he would expect if he took his car in for servicing, otherwise they might as well dispense with the bill altogether and simply have the waiter announce, 'That'll be £35.95, service not included.'

Now here's where I let the side down. Having said all that, I have to confess that I hardly ever check my bill, unless the total is so astronomical that it's evident a mistake has been made and I've been charged for the next table's lobsters. If I do happen to check it, it's only out of pique because I've had a rotten lunch or bad service. I know I should, for whenever I do add up the bill it nearly always turns out to be a couple of pounds out in the restaurant's favour, which I charitably put down to bad maths induced by work-pressure and near-total illegibility. But running a ballpoint down a list of prices while one's guest gazes ostentatiously at a potted plant seems bad manners to me, particularly if it involves cross-questioning the waiter on what that 1 mb du 3.95 might be when it's at home. Rather than end a pleasant lunch on this dismal note, I pay the bill without fuss and pocket it, checking it later if I think it was on the high side. If I find it outrageously over what it should be, I drop the restaurant from my list.

Correction: one circumstance in which I will always scrutinise the bill most carefully is when I've ordered something that never arrived. Almost invariably, the hiccup in the system that caused a breakdown in communication between my table and the kitchen turns out to have circumnavigated the accounts desk.

The Tip

I WAS IN a Miami bar presided over by a barman built like a truck when in came a character evidently on holiday from the Bronx, who plonked down a package-tour coupon entitling him to a free drink.

He got the drink, knocked it back and made to leave. The aggrieved barman, searching in vain for his expected quarter tip, yelled after him: 'Hey! Gratooity!'

The freeloader snarled over his shoulder, 'So what's twenny per cent of nuthin'?'

Twenty per cent of nothing is the same as fifteen per cent, twelve and a half per cent or ten per cent of nothing. It is when we come to percentages of something that the trouble sets in.

Waiters reckon that we tend to be less generous with our tips at lunchtime than at dinnertime, the scientific explanation being that we are more likely to be drunk after dinner. For myself, I feel that a good lunch properly presented deserves a good tip. I am not averse to over-tipping if the occasion warrants it, any more than I am against any other form of personal extravagance so long as it does not descend into vulgarity. But in the general run of things I reckon fifteen per cent is about right, though twelve and a half is still acceptable in most places. Twenty per cent - the norm now in many New York and West Coast restaurants - is too high. Ten per cent, a figure I shall come back to in a moment, is too low.

But fifteen per cent of what? One thing I am mean about is paying a proportion of the bill's Value Added Tax as a gratuity. Now that VAT is always built into the menu prices, any restaurant bill represents 115 per cent of the true cost of the meal. A fifteen per cent tip on such a total is therefore, in reality, 17.25 per cent. On a fifty pound bill including VAT, that means a tip of £7.50

[56]

ℭ THE TIP ℭ

instead of the proper figure of £6.50. Why should anyone want to tip a pound to a VAT registration number?

If the VAT were itemised separately, it would show the fifteen per cent tipper at a glance what he should leave – just as in New York, where one can simply double the eight per cent sales tax listed on the check. With VAT concealed in the total, quite a complicated sum is necessary – divide by 23 to produce five per cent of the price without VAT, then multiply by three to produce fifteen per cent. If that's beyond you after a large brandy or you feel that tapping your pocket calculator might throw a shadow between you and your lunch companion, just leave twelve and a half per cent which is as near as dammit fifteen per cent in real terms.

Now what about 'Service included'? If it's twelve and a half per cent, as it usually is, it's invariably on a total which includes VAT, so they're getting not far short of fifteen per cent really, which is all you need to leave unless you feel like adding a pound or two as a gesture of appreciation.

If it's ten per cent then it's neither one thing nor the other, as the waiter will make clear when asked if service is included. 'Service is included at ten per cent, sir,' he will say pointedly – a euphemism, and quite right too, for 'Up to a point, sir.' So, anxious not to appear stingy, you add another five per cent to the compound sum and in your mathematical haziness bring it up to rather more than you would have wanted to tip if left to your own devices. Not satisfactory, and I wish that Wheeler's for instance, whose splendidly plush seafront Sheridan and nearby sister establishment in Brighton often see me attacking a lunchtime sole, would either include a realistic service charge or leave it to the customer.

Two pesky little restaurant habits jar when it comes to tipping. One is the waiter not bringing back the change. Even though you meant him to keep it, it's not for him to assume so (and for all he knows you might have intended to add a few bob, so he could be the loser). The other is the avaricious practice of leaving the bottom line of a credit card slip blank, even though a hefty tip is included. Fill in the total and don't add a penny.

On the subject of tipping by credit card, though, the staff in some places do have a grievance. They claim that the service charge you write in goes to head office and is never seen again. Even if it's not entirely true, should you hear the complaint voiced no harm can come of tipping in cash if possible.

The whole subject of tipping puts a lot of people's backs up. Some feel that it should be abolished and restaurant staff paid a decent wage. Cromwell, I'm sure, would have felt the same – had he allowed the restaurants to remain open.

My own feeling is that the ceremony, properly conducted, brings the meal to a satisfactory end. Dispensing a fat tip after a good lunch can bring as rosy a glow to the bosom as imbibing a large brandy. One feels, if not like a millionaire for a day, at least like a millionaire for a minute. And there is always the hope, usually unfulfilled, that one's lunch companion will be impressed.

But the true purpose of the tip is neither to massage one's own ego nor to provide new shoes for the chef de partie's baby. Calling it a service charge distorts its simple object which is to express thanks for personal attention received. No, you do not tip the shop assistant but then the shop assistant does not dance attendance upon you up to thirty or forty times for a single sale.

A lunch without wine, the Italians are fond of saying, is like a woman without breasts. A lunch without an adequate tip is like a man without his wallet.

But it really should be earned. On a trip to Cairo, I noticed that most of the big restaurants employ someone to hang around by the exit accepting gratuities. He appears to have no other function. We don't have that system here but I do sometimes think, when adding service when there has been very little of it, 'So *this* is what twenny per cent of nuthin' is.'

Indigestifs

The menu that does not materialise.

The menu that materialises but is not followed up by someone to take the order after an appropriate interval.

The menu that is accompanied by a hovering waiter with his order pad.

The wine list that does not arrive.

The wine list that arrives but in the sommelier's belief, apparently, that you wish to read it as literature, since he makes no attempt to resume contact.

The sommelier whose eye you cannot catch.

The bottle which is dumped on your table unopened after it has been presented for your approval.

The salt which is not on the table. The bread which you have to ask for – twice.

The waiter who interrupts your punchline with 'Who's having the avocado mousse?'

The sommelier who, to make up for his earlier low profile, now bobs up to refill your glasses after every sip.

The waiter who says 'This is not my table – I'll tell your waiter' when you've asked for bread three times. But he doesn't.

The canneloni that arrives when you've asked for crespolini, and the waiter says 'I can change it if you like,' and you feel obliged to say 'No, I'm sure it's delicious,' but it isn't.

The five minute interval between the arrival of your meal and that of your lunch companion.

The main course that arrives incomplete so that you have to ask again for the vegetable you've already ordered, and the flustered waiter says 'Iss coming, iss coming' but you know and he knows that he's forgotten, and the *petits pois* arrive just in time to accompany your last mouthful of chicken.

The pudding trolley that is wheeled up while you are still prodding a morsel of veal out of your hollow tooth.

The dirty plates that are not cleared away by a waiter passing empty-handed.

The dirty plates that remain on the table even after he has come to ask if you would like coffee.

The missing ashtray.

The waiter who says 'One minute, sir' when you attract his attention, then puts you totally out of his mind.

The coffee that has to be asked for again after it's been ordered and the cups have been brought to the table.

After all this, the waiter fetching up at your table unbidden, completing the bill, and slapping it on the table without a word.

Eating On T' Street

A STORY PURLOINED FROM my book *Waterhouse At Large*:

Capri. An open-air terrace restaurant in the shade of an orange grove. A perfect day. The scent of bougainvillaea mingles delicately with the aroma of canneloni.

A Yorkshire couple pause and study the menu. Below the expanse of white tablecloths is a steeply-sloping vineyard, and far below the harbour is the Bay of Naples, and far away on the shimmering horizon, like a brushstroke in a Chinese picture, is a smudge of purple which is Vesuvius.

The lady tugs her husband's sleeve.

'Come on, Ronnie – you don't want to eat out in t' street.'

In my household the experience of lunching out of doors has ever since been known as eating out in t' street.

Eating out in t' street – or on t' terrace, or in t' garden – adds a whole new dimension to lunch. Also on Capri I remember lunching in a garden where the response to a request for lemon was to pick one from the tree under whose branches our table was set. It lent enchantment to an already memorable lunch.

The experience is a rare one in England – and an even rarer one in America, where an indoor garden in an air-conditioned atrium is their idea of alfresco dining (Exception: brunch on the patio of the Polo Lounge at the Beverly Hills Hotel, where the crickets on a balmy summer's day perform better than a Palm Court orchestra). The few places with eating on t' street facilities – there are more than there were, and there would

✄ THE THEORY & PRACTICE OF LUNCH ✄

be more still if the authorities did not take the view that enjoyment constitutes an obstruction and a health and safety hazard – quite properly reserve their outdoor tables for their regulars on those few days of the year when the sun has got his hat on and is coming out to lunch. The one and only good reason for plugging ourselves into Europe, so far as I am concerned, was the possibility that we might take up eating like Europeans, but we are a long time getting round to it. Perhaps the climate is against us but even where the outdoors has a roof over its head we don't take up the opportunity. The City of Leeds, for example (which admittedly boasts the happily bustling La Terrazza, my invariable lunch stop when back in my home town) has finer arcades than Milan's, but not a restaurant in any one of them. And what about our railway stations? Perhaps it is asking too much of St Pancras to emulate the terracotta caverns of the Oyster Bar in Grand Central, or Waterloo the fabled Train Bleu restaurant overlooking the Gare de Lyon; but those great empty concourses are crying out for café tables and a brasserie menu.

But to return to earth, or only one flight of steps up from it: the first floor terrace at the Meridiana, a breath of the Mediterranean on Fulham Road (if you close your eyes and drink in the diesel fumes you could be in Naples) is one place I would aim for on a hot Sunday, always the best day for eating out of doors, if it weren't milling with Sloane Rangers (I thought they were all supposed to be down in the country at weekends?). When I lived in Islington, Frederick's in Camden Passage was a summer haunt – although it isn't open on Sunday the garden makes it feel like Sunday – but trying to follow the sun from SW5 to N1 is as futile an expedition as trying to find the end of the rainbow. So at the first sign of a heatwave I sprint round to Pontevecchio on the Old Brompton Road, which has a big pavement area protected by an awning and removable plastic window partitions in the manner of a Paris boulevard café – a sensibly malleable arrangement enabling them to deal with any act of treachery the English weather may care

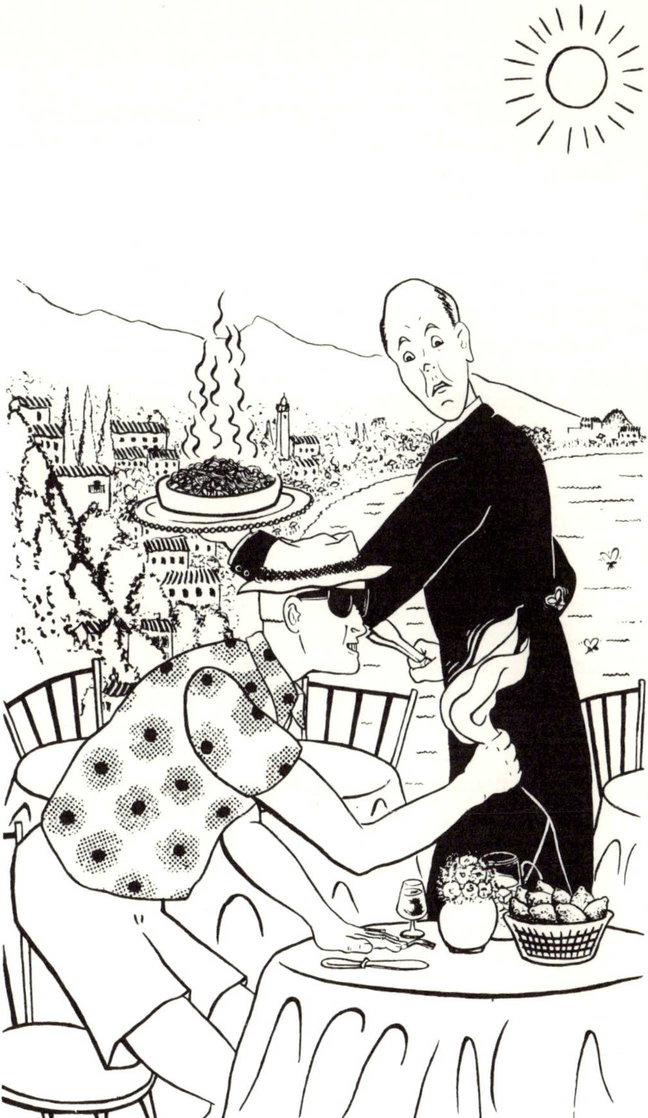

THE THEORY & PRACTICE OF LUNCH

to try on. You can sip your Campari, fiddle with your breadsticks, and watch the world go by (and in salubrious Earl's Court, going by is what you hope the world will keep on doing).

Eating out in t' street makes lunch feel like a holiday, for the good and obvious reason that it was while on holiday that most of us learned the pleasures and pitfalls of taking lunch out of doors.

The main pitfalls are the weather and the wasps.

If it's too cold to eat outside, the intelligence will be signalled the moment you arrive by the fact that everyone else is eating inside. Value their judgement. Even if Michael Fish was right and the sun does come out in due course, it can be pretty forlorn being the only outdoor customers. Your (indoors) waiter will regard you as an adjunct or afterthought and you will feel neglected. If you do opt for out of doors and a single raindrop plops into your chilled vichyssoise, apply for a transfer indoors instantly. Do the same if you've misjudged the temperature and it's nippier than you thought. Grinning and bearing it has no part in lunch.

Wasps you can do nothing about beyond spraying yourself with insect repellant and not ordering the fruit flan. Do not flail out at them with your napkin, or when you come to try to attract the waiter's attention he will think you are trying to kill wasps. Take solace in the fact that any establishment frequented by wasps is likely to be of the highest quality, particularly in ambience. They are quite choosy, you know.

The pleasures of lunching out of doors are that each experience of it becomes a picture postcard of itself; that there is a good deal more to look at than there is inside; that the service is pleasantly relaxed and leisurely (what might be an intolerable delay inside the restaurant seems a civilised interval for sipping wine and contemplating the passing show when outside of it); that a lazy summer benevolence flavours the whole meal like a sprinkling of herbs; that on top of that the open air wafting the aromas about makes the food taste even tastier, particularly if it's been charcoal grilled; that if the wine is liquid sunshine

EATING ON T'STREET

then the sun is ethereal wine; that the essential naughtiness of lunch is heightened by the fact of one's lunching in dark glasses; and that the nearer one gets to the coffee stage, the more attractive seems the idea of a siesta.

Eat and drink as if you were in the South of France. If indeed you *are* in the south of France, so much the better.

Brasseries

The brasserie, which so far as this country is concerned thrived in Edwardian times and then went into eclipse for about sixty years, is so perfect a vehicle for lunch that it is amazing how serious lunch companions – and even more, frivolous lunch companions – managed to live without the institution for so long. Perhaps they made do on sandwiches.

The essence of a brasserie is that you should be able to walk in off the street and order what you like, from a toasted sandwich to a four course meal: thus it fulfils one important definition of lunch which is that it should be a meal where you eat what you please while dinner is a meal where you eat what you think you're supposed to have. The constant turnover of customers creates that atmosphere of hubbub which is as a whiff of oxygen to the jaded lunch companion. There is, too, a raffishly foreign feeling to a brasserie which gives it just that required air of mild sin. Not for every occasion, of course – if your aim is to whisper sweet nothings you had better choose some place where you don't need a megaphone – but in the right mood, the brasserie is perfect for lunch companionship.

In any foreign city (see *Playing away*) I would always head for a buzzing brasserie if serendipity and the smell of fish soup didn't lead me elsewhere. In this country, brasseries are still hard to find outside the capital (Bristol, for some reason, is a great exception), but London now seems to have them by the score (though Langan's, which calls itself a brasserie, is really a restaurant, while Kettner's, which calls itself a restaurant, is really a brasserie).

Brasseries are essentially neighbourhood or works canteens, so there is no point in crossing town to one.

BRASSERIES

The three I use most are Kettner's, the Soho Brasserie in Old Compton Street (where lunch companions 'just popping out for an hour' stay for two) and La Brasserie on the Brompton Road, a favourite on Sundays when I like to arrive just as the lunch crowd are taking over from the breakfast crowd – an exercise not unlike one battalion relieving another on the battle lines.

[68]

Ever On Sunday

SIX DAYS SHALT thou labour, and on the seventh shalt thou have lunch.

This is not to say that you will have passed lunch by during the week; but lunch on Sunday should be something special.

True, there is not quite that deliciously improper feeling of doing something one really shouldn't – especially among married persons now lunching with their wives or husbands instead of their lovers – but this tendency towards tameness is amply compensated for by the knowledge that while one is slurping down wine and getting garlic butter on one's chin, the lawn goes unmowed, the car unwashed, and the briefcase full of homework unlooked at.

Sunday lunch has a life of its own. It tends to be more boisterous, more disorganised, more spur of the moment than weekday lunch. Like *Brunch* (see below) it is often an occasion for family and friends rather than for couples – the bigger the family and the more the friends the better. Many couples do like to eat out on Sundays, of course, but this is when they are most likely to link up with other couples to become foursomes or sixsomes.

Sunday lunch is best taken at some easy-going place where a long table can be infinitely extended and more and more places laid as lunch companions A and B reel in from the pub with the announcement that they have just bumped into dear C and D who would love to join the party if nobody minds them bringing little e who will be as good as gold. (She won't, so best find an establishment that likes children. The Italians dote on them, but please don't take advantage of their amiability by letting little e and that hyperactive little f play chariot

THE THEORY & PRACTICE OF LUNCH

races with the hors d'oeuvres trolley. Children should be given some bread to play with and taught to be good little lunch companions. This does not, by the way, entail them eating up on pain of getting no pudding. Anyone taking kids to a restaurant and then depriving them of their *raison d'être* for being there should be reported to the NSPCC by the pastry chef.)

It has to be said that not all lunch companions like the proximity of large family groups. Those who like to keep themselves to themselves would do best to stick to the *Brasseries* (see under that heading) where lunch parties are likelier to come in packs of two or four. But for those whose enjoyment of lunch is only enhanced by the sight (and sound) of others enjoying theirs, a noisy family restaurant, even though they may be childless orphans themselves, is a pleasurable resort indeed.

The definitive Sunday family lunch establishment, so far as I'm concerned, is La Favorita in Sorrento, which is not so much a restaurant as a culinary stadium, arranged in terraces like an indoor vineyard. The reason it is so huge becomes clear as the place begins to fill up after Mass and whole dynasties troop in to settle themselves around tables for ten, twelve, sixteen, twenty – three or four generations of them, wispy matriarchs all in black, family godfathers stubble-chinned and without collar or tie to their serge suits, barrel-chested married sons and plump daughters-in-law in their Sunday best, teenagers in jeans and sneakers, bambinos got up like pageboys and maids of honour, and all so deferential to one another as, in strict order of precedence, they pass around the mineral water and the wine and the olive oil and help their seniors to salad and sample one another's pasta and seafood. If through some medical condition – it would have to be terminal – I were no longer allowed the indulgence of Sunday lunch, I should gladly pay a substantial cover charge for a potted palm to stand behind in order to feast my eyes, if not my belly, on Sunday lunch at La Favorita – a cross, in its polite rituals observed in an atmosphere clamouring with exuberance, between the Japanese tea ceremony and a carnival.

EVER ON SUNDAY

A little nearer to home, I find welcome evidence at the Hungry Horse in the Fulham Road that family life is not dead, though it may well be comatose after the steak and kidney pie. At Joe Allen's, theatrical folk and journalists who use the place as their canteen during the week take their families there on Sundays. The menu here is more brunchlike than lunchlike, which brings us neatly to the allied subject of –

Brunch

THE AMERICANS, WHO invented it, serve the best brunch. Or rather, you serve it yourself, since the very best brunch is a buffet affair. On either side of the Atlantic, a hotel rather than a regular restaurant is where you are likeliest to track down the authentic article, though some London hotels try to pass off their everyday carvery service as a brunch, which it isn't unless augmented by the kind of offerings you would expect to find under the chafing dishes on a country house sideboard when coming down to breakfast.

True brunch does have to be breakfast-based – eggy things, bacon, sausages, French toast, kedgeree – though with a civil nod towards lunch by way of hams and roast cuts, and a strong leaning towards afternoon tea in the shape of pastries and gooey puds. Croissants and other breads must be in evidence (if you are in New York, when you should be brunching to the sound of Cole Porter's piano at the Waldorf Astoria, there will be blueberry muffins too) as must Dutch and Danish cheeses, salamis, fresh fruits and juices.

Brunch is to be consumed only on a Sunday, kicking off ideally at twelve sharp with a Bloody Mary or Bucks Fizz, the only drink permissible thereafter being champagne, with or without the orange juice. (But beware any brunch establishment promising unlimited champagne inclusive. Unlimited champagne is usually served at strictly limited intervals.)

Unlike lunch in general, brunch in particular is more for family and friends than for twosomes. Children love it: they feel very grown up trotting off to the buffet all by themselves to pile their plates high with nursery food.

The most leisurely and informal of lunching experiences, brunch has something of the atmosphere of home – if only home had a Palm Court breakfast room with a

BRUNCH

string trio. The Sunday papers may be perused between trips to the groaning board (the place loses points if your dirty plate hasn't been removed by the time you return to the table: why should self-service result in the bare-minimal waiter service required being so often slaphappy?), but it is far more entertaining simply to loll around and observe the passing show. Brunch is always attended by legions of greedygutses and it is quite fun for the children to keep tally of the number of times that stout gentleman has been up to the hotplate and how many pastries that lady with the chins has so far consumed.

There will also be a good deal of joshing about one's own party's intake. Brunch is the one form of lunch where it is quite in order to gorge oneself. The idea is to emulate a buffet-powered camel, taking on board enough provender to last until Monday morning. Certainly, if you can look even so much as a cheese sandwich in the face at supper time, you will not have done justice to your brunch.

It is lunch at its most hedonistic and for some, apt to be tinged with guilt. Those with a puritanical streak should make a point of starting with the stewed prunes.

Home Cooking

THE FIRST THING to be said about giving a lunch party at home is that it should not be reciprocal. Paying back social debts – or old scores – is the function of dinner. So is the bringing together of two couples who hopefully will find much in common over the sherry. I have attended many very agreeable formal luncheon parties of this description. Pleasant they were, but lunch in our sense they were not. They were in reality dinner parties with a daylight curfew.

Lunch at home, while clearly it has to be prepared for, and advance notice must be given of it, should seem an altogether more impromptu affair. While I have said that true lunch at home is not pot luck, it should give the impression of so being, though the pot has to be a very large one with a good deal of something tasty bubbling away in it. The event should feature a mixture of family and friends, with children and dogs in evidence for preference. It should start at noon and go on till six. (Sunday is the only day for a lunch party at home.) If it is possible for it to be staged in the garden, then in the garden it should be staged. If not, then around a huge kitchen table. The dining room, by my definition, is for dinner. But it is the table that is the essential item. You do not want your lunch companions sprawling about on cushions and beanbags, balancing plates of boeuf Strogonoff on their laps and chatting only to those they happen to be sharing a corner with. What you have there is an indoor picnic. True lunch at home is a communion: it should involve everybody present with everybody else in a crossfire of talk and laughter.

A fact of life about having a group of friends round for lunch is that someone's car is going to break down,

HOME COOKING

someone else is going to lose their way, someone's child will have had a nose-bleed upon setting off, and someone will be just congenitally late. The wine, meanwhile, will be flowing so enjoyably (it should be plonk, and lots of it) that it is two o'clock before you know it. What you want, then, is a stew or casserole or something of that order that will happily wait until everybody is ready for it. Put everything on the table, with the afters and cheese on the Welsh dresser, and leave your lunch companions to get on with it, either helping themselves or one another. Don't bother with starters, but have a big bowl of salad which they can dive into before, during or after, as they please. Station bottles of wine at either end of the table, in the middle too if it's big enough, and let them pour it themselves. Children are allowed watered wine. They are also allowed to clear away plates. After two helpings of pudding, or one helping each of two puddings, they can be sent out into the garden to play or upstairs to watch something unsuitable on video, while your grown-up lunch companions get on with their wine, cheese and coffee. If at least one of your guests doesn't go off for a quiet potter in the garden, only to be discovered half an hour later fast asleep in a deckchair, the lunch cannot be judged an unqualified success.

The case for lunching at home is that it's considerably cheaper than taking eight people to a restaurant (does anyone, any more, except on the company, ever take more than two people to a restaurant?), that you can start and end the proceedings when you feel like it, and that children are welcome, including the baby who can be dumped upstairs in a carrycot. It may even be, also, that the food is better than you are likely to get outside. At all events, entertaining a bunch of favourite lunch companions at home is a hugely satisfying experience, though so exhausting that next Sunday you really ought to treat yourselves to a quiet lunch for two at that very nice place round the corner.

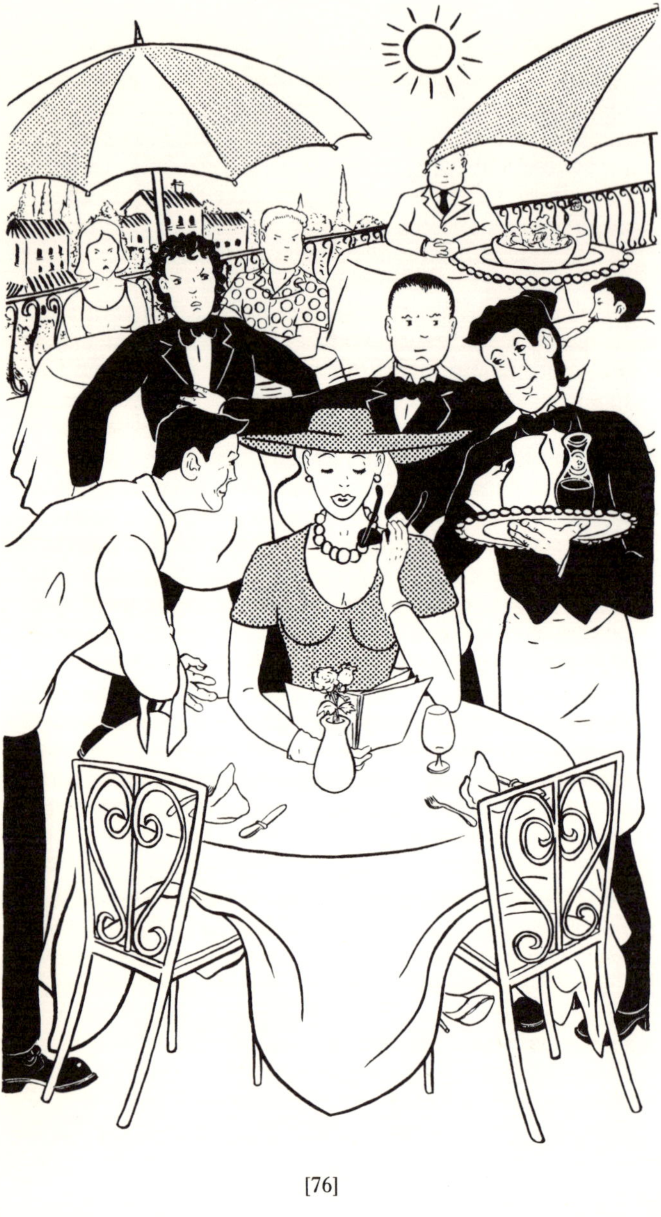

Luncheon For One Please, James

Just as many wives will not bother to cook for themselves when their husbands are away, but will make do with something out of a tin, so many lunch companions well used to feeding their faces congenially will settle for pub grub, sandwiches or even junk food when compelled by circumstances to lunch by themselves.

The lone lunch companion, if the term is not a paradox, is more commonly to be sighted on the continent and in the United States than here – perhaps because the demolition gangs and refurbishers have left us with far fewer no-nonsense feet-on-the-ground businessmen's restaurants where a man (or a woman) may feel at home with only a chump chop, a half bottle and the *Times* crossword for company. (When the royalties from this little volume come pouring in, I am going to open a franchise chain of chop-houses and clean up.) Seafood restaurants such as Manzi's in Leicester Street or English's in Brighton, where one can perch at a marble counter over a dozen oysters and a Black Velvet or two, are where once is likeliest to encounter the lone lunch companion these days.

Though the occasion may be tinged with self-pitying melancholy, a proper lunch alone in a decent restaurant must have the edge on a scratch lunch in an uncomfortable, crowded sandwich bar. It is a course I particularly recommend to the jilted lover, always provided that the restaurant of his choice is the one now used by his former consort and her current escort, and that his haunted, reproachful countenance falls within her range of vision whenever she picks up her glass of wine ('Ah, yes! The Frascati we always used to drink together at the flat!')

✍ THE THEORY & PRACTICE OF LUNCH ✎

She may not enjoy her lunch but he certainly will, for all that he had better not have the pudding if she is to be persuaded that he is pining unto death.

This scenario can of course be reversed, with her tears plopping into her Perrier while he makes a sweating try at looking as if he is not even with his latest in lunch paramours, let alone that the reason the greedy pig is handling her T-bone steak with a fork is that she is groping him under the tablecloth with her other hand. This brings us to lone female lunch companions. Legend has it that they are patronised, pestered and even pawed by (particularly Italian) waiters. My own observation is that women lunching alone are usually very civilly treated, the manager or maître d' making a point of seeing that everything is going smoothly for them. This may be condescending on his part but they should be so lucky: there are people who lunch twice a week for a year in the same restaurant without benefitting from that kind of attention.

I have myself become a lone lunch companion only in recent years. Coming from the puritanical north I for long thought it vaguely immoral and wasteful to eat out alone. I still feel it's wasteful in the sense that I would rather be occupying my time with an engaging companion. But these days, if out and about and left to my own devices at the witching hour of one, I would sooner have my feet under a restaurant table than my elbows on a pub bar. I arm myself with a magazine or newspaper (*Private Eye*, the *Spectator* and the London *Standard* are the best restaurant reads) but usually the floorshow that is as integral to lunch as the cabaret is to a night-club supper is diversion enough between courses. Indeed, I sometimes wonder during my unilateral lunch interval at Val Ceno's in Fleet Street or Jules Bar in Jermyn Street, how lunchtime theatre ever caught on when lunch itself is theatre.

Playing Away

LUNCHING OUTSIDE ONE'S own territory can present problems. If we're talking about this country, and you're away on business, then you're likely to put yourself in the hands of your local contacts who will carry you off either to a converted mill where Giles does the cooking while Emma serenely presides over what so much looks like her private dining room that you will be made to feel that nobody is paying, or to the local prawn cocktail and steak outlet which may be good of its kind, or not. Anyway, business lunch is not lunch. If you're on holiday, on honeymoon or just having a day out, and you're in virgin territory, then you'll probably go by personal recommendation or the *Good Food Guide*. If the area you're in has been declared persona non grata by the *Guide*, tough. Even if it hasn't, you may be missing out on a first-class restaurant. In Newcastle a few weeks ago, I was taken to one of the best places I have eaten in this year, the Fisherman's Wharf. Not a peep about it in the *Good Food Guide* (and not, alas, open for lunch). I wish that some philanthropic organisation or other, recognising that a hungry traveller finding himself in, let's say Fleetwood, has got to eat whether the local mushroom and truffle sauce has lumps in it or not, would compile a Domesday Book of all the restaurants in Britain and let the punter decide for himself. (Actually, if you *should* find yourself in Fleetwood, go to the Trafalgar, an unpretentious little restaurant where you will eat better than in any of the grand hotels in Blackpool, and say I sent you.)

Abroad, of course, is easier, but even in France and Italy it is possible to get one's feet under the wrong table. I shall never forget the horror of a lunch in one of the

THE THEORY & PRACTICE OF LUNCH

nicest-looking trattorias in Naples which was, however, totally deserted when my party arrived. Soon it dawned upon us, from the listless, demoralised demeanour of the staff, that it was likely still to be totally deserted when we left. And so it proved, as the reason for its emptiness also made itself manifest – we'd picked the one restaurant in Naples that couldn't cook pasta.

Both at home and away, I recommend the seek-and-find techniques developed on a lunching holiday a few years ago, when a lunch companion and I managed to take lunch in five different countries in five days. Basing ourselves in Brussels and armed with the Thomas Cook timetable, we lunched on successive days in Amsterdam, Cologne, Luxembourg, Paris and Ostend. Only in Paris, where we headed straight for the Train Bleu restaurant in the Gare de Lyon, did we know where we were going before we set off. (Since we were whisked there by Metro from the Gare du Nord, and wished to devote every minute of our tightly-scheduled stay to that Versailles-like eating palace, we did not actually set foot in the streets of Paris on that trip.) Elsewhere – nudged, it's true, by the Michelin guides – we simply ambled about until we found a likely-looking place, and then, noses pressed to the window like the Bisto kids, applied certain tests.

Is the place a lunch restaurant at heart, as distinct from a dinner restaurant? There is such a division, just as there is between day people and night people. Lunch restaurants tend to have more of a no-nonsense air about them – white (not pink or blue) cloths and napery, an absence of candles and flowers, a coat-stand rather than a cloakroom girl. (This, of course, is a generalisation: there are many restaurants which successfully operate as both.)

Is it professionally run – in other words, not by amateurs doing it for fun if it's in Britain (it's always more fun for them than it is for the customers) and not by incompetents if it's abroad? Watch the owner or maître d'. If he is incapable of passing an empty table without straightening a knife or removing a dirty plate, then he's a professional who will have trained his staff like a sergeant-major.

Is it going to be pleasantly full, not forlornly empty? If there's a basket of bread already laid on each table, the glasses are not turned upside down and the waiters look happy, they're anticipating a good day.

Does the menu feature a down-to-earth *prix fixe* section? If so, it has a sound coterie of regulars – always good for atmosphere.

Finally, you will remember our words on the Lone Lunch Companion. Is there a man sitting alone at a corner table, chomping his way through three courses with his newspaper propped against a bottle of wine? I don't know why it should be so, since he is not lunching in our sense of the word but merely eating lunch, but the lone lunch companion is a near-infallible sign that one is in for a good experience.

Getting It Regular

IT WOULD BE very unwise of two lunch companions to make a voyage into the unknown by venturing into a restaurant neither of them has set foot in before. Which is not to say they should never try anywhere new – but the usual form is for the host, if not the guest, to be familiar with the place already. This being the pattern, it follows that most if not all lunch companions may be classified as regulars at a handful of restaurants.

Regulars have certain rights and certain duties, and in turn the restaurants they frequent have certain obligations towards them.

Regular lunch companions have a right to their usual table if they happen to have asked for it first (regulars can never comprehend that their especial table, like a wayward mistress, has other favourites whom it entertains in their absence). If the place is full and they arrive unexpectedly, they have a right to be squeezed in somewhere if that's at all possible. They do not, however, have the right to hi-jack someone else's reserved table, nor to make neglecting to book a habit.

They should not expect to be fawned over but they are entitled to expect to be made a little fuss of – everybody enjoys that, both the fussers and the fussed. They may expect their order to be taken by the guv'nor himself rather than a minion, and for him to keep a special eye on their table to see that everything is going smoothly.

In return, they should be more tolerant of the occasional cock-up than they might be in a strange restaurant where like a critic at a play they may legitimately claim that whatever has gone wrong backstage is none of their business, it being the performance alone on which they make their judgement. In a place familiar

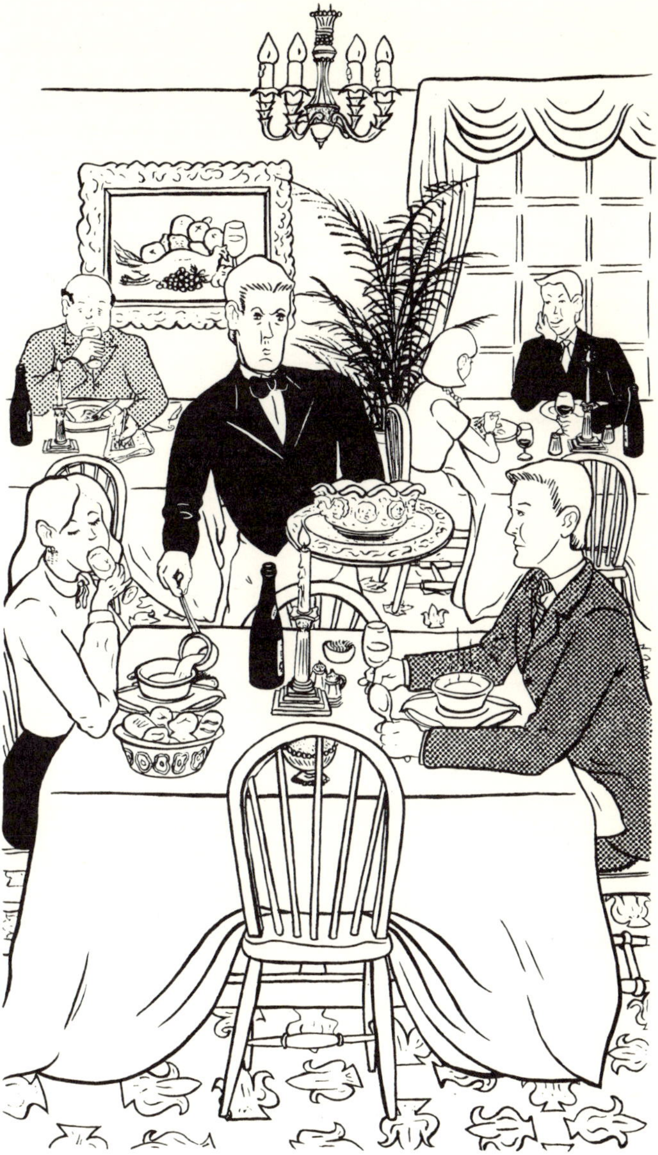

to them, lunch companions will gradually become aware of the snags in the system – the fact that the serving hatch is badly positioned, the hors d'oeuvres trolley is too wide to manoeuvre through the tables without difficulty, the cashier is ga-ga, the wine waiter's arthritis is playing him up – and make allowances. True lunch companions are more than happy to put up with less than perfect service – being privy to professional problems makes them feel part of the family, far more than they are ever likely to be in any of those amateurish husband-and-wife converted stables which boast of making their guests feel 'at home.'

Regulars have an obligation to recommend their favourite restaurant to selected friends, and if the place is going through a bad patch as the best of restaurants is inclined to do from time to time for no discernible reason, they have a duty to lend it their support a little more frequently than usual.

For their part, the management should treat their regulars as valued customers, not as old friends who won't mind if they don't get their wine as promptly as usual once they learn that Carlo is off with his arthritis. They will not, it goes without saying, blink an eyelid when someone who has been habitually coming in with a brunette lunch companion suddenly appears with a redhead lunch companion; yet neither will they, should he eventually resume his lunching status quo, thereafter leer at him conspiratorially while ladling out the soup.

Should a regular give them a miss for a few weeks, they should not receive him with a pained expression and a reproachful cry of 'We haven't seen you for so long, we thought you were dead!' (to which the only possible reply is 'Yes, I nearly was – it was that turbot you gave me'). I can think of three or four restaurants formerly on my circuit whose thresholds I will no longer cross because they used to make such a song and dance if I didn't patronise them for a while. On the other hand, when I walked into Chez Victor for the first time in about twelve years (nothing they'd said: it was just that a former lunch companion always used to take me there and when

GETTING IT REGULAR

we lost touch I took up other places with other people, as one tends to do) they greeted me with a casually welcoming 'Nice to see you again' and we resumed our old relationship like a glove.

Regulars are not unpartial to a drink on the house from time to time, but this should not be a signal for the boss to join them at their table unless specifically invited (and not even then unless business is unusually slack), particularly if he is going to talk about his problems with the VAT inspector or even worse, the health inspector.

Regulars make a sound contribution to any restaurant, and not only to its profits. The ambience, of which I speak elsewhere, is helped enormously by the fact of a handful of lunch companions dotted about who find the place so congenial and relaxing that they want to return to it again and again. This has an accumulative effect in that it adds so much to the general air of enjoyment that all the other lunch companions resolve to become regulars too.

Dress

THESE ARE CASUAL times we live in, but lunch eaten in a vest is not lunch at all: it is a slow-motion fast food snack consumed at a table instead of on the hoof along the Earls Court Road.

Though I am unlikely ever to be voted one of the Ten Best Dressed Men I always make a point of wearing a collar and tie for lunch, and I prefer my lunch companion, if male, to do the same, or if female, to dress as if she considers the occasion to be an occasion. This is not out of respect for the food – I should find it difficult to be deferential towards a dead fish – but partly out of respect for one another; partly because the effort a restaurant puts into pleasing its customers should be backed up to a small degree by some effort from them; but mainly because in any restaurant all the lunch companions are part of the scenery. If the people at the next table look as if they have just come up out of the drains, it is like being at one of those avant-garde Shakespearian productions where Hamlet walks on in dungarees.

These days few restaurants outside the four-star class are going to throw anybody out for not wearing a tie, and indeed many of them encourage informality by being themselves informal. Where the waiters dress like out-of-work actors (they *are* out-of-work actors), then I concede there is no obligation upon lunch companions to dress as if off to collect their OBE at Buckingham Palace. Where the staff are still got up like penguins, however, it is clear, even though they are letting in sartorial riff-raff in order to fill their tables, that they secretly pine for higher dress standards from their customers. It is wrong, and unlunchcompanionable, to impose leather bomber jackets and sweat shirts on an establishment in a spirit

DRESS

of take it or leave it simply because it's plain they need the business.

The dress rule should be – wear not what you yourself feel most comfortable in, but what will make your fellow lunch companions and the people who serve you feel most comfortable. Which, to anyone with the sensitivity of the true lunch companion, should amount to one and the same thing.

For my part, I shall continue to wear my tie. Where else should I collect my soup stains?

Care and Training Of Waiters

*A*SKED WHO MAKES the best waiters, a restaurateur friend of mine replied 'Waiters.' With less brevity, the manager of the Café Pelican, that little bit of Montparnasse in St Martin's Lane, made much the same point to a journalist: 'I don't want students, they don't care about the customers. I want people who want to be waiters all their lives.'

Resting actors may act at being waiters and students may play at being waiters, and very good many of them are at their dressing-up games; but there is no substitute for a real, professional waiter.

A real waiter never walks past his tables empty-handed without scanning each one to see whether anything is needed or has to be cleared away. Customers do not have to catch his eye: he catches theirs. Compare with the amateur, who may well deliver an order without mishap, but who makes no attempt to perform any task on his way back to the serving-hatch, and who sees so little out of the corner of his eye that he might as well be in blinkers.

A real waiter can store six separate lunch orders in his head and carry six loaded plates in his arms; and what is more, deliver them to the right people at the right tables. Should he make a mistake, it is a calamity, not a giggle.

A real waiter is trained. If in America, where some of the best waiters are to be found (especially in the old-fashioned bar and grill establishments where they still wear the traditional white shirt, black tie and white tablecloth around the waist) he will have started as a busboy, restricted to laying and clearing tables. It is an

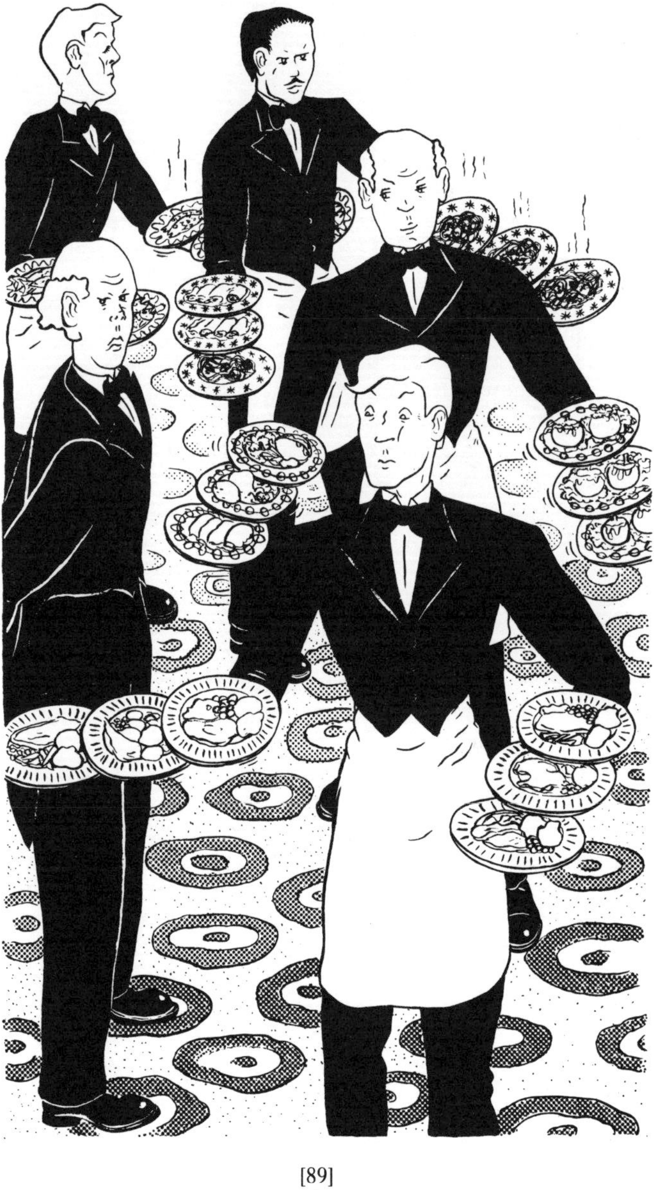

THE THEORY & PRACTICE OF LUNCH

apprenticeship system we could do with here. But the alternative form of training – enduring a bullying owner who first tells the fledgling waiter what he has to do and then bites his head off every time he doesn't do it, isn't half bad either.

A real waiter will be able to describe every dish on the menu on request, open a bottle of champagne without spilling a drop and a bottle of still wine without splitting the cork, and thieve a side salad from under a colleague's nose if he feels that his own customer's need for it is greater.

A real waiter knows when to bring the black pepper without being asked.

A real waiter dresses like a proper waiter and not like an art teacher or a Gay Nineties saloon-bar keeper.

A real waiter is a walking fountain of reassurance. No, he hasn't forgotten the toast for your pâté but because you're afraid he may have done he takes it upon himself to assure you that it's on its way, swallowing the implicit slur on his professionalism.

A real waiter is not servile but he does not go in for badinage – the telltale sign of the amateur waiter who has to prove that he is cut out for something better than waiting at table. Opening a bottle of champagne efficiently enough, a waiter who in real life was a design student or something of the sort said to me as I studied my brasserie menu, 'The cork should pop as discreetly as a duchess passing wind.' It was not what I wanted to hear at lunch.

A real waiter is not necessarily French or Italian. Contrary to myth, the English not only make good waiters but very many of them *are* good waiters, notably at the great hotels where they make their guests feel that they have won a butler in a raffle.

Real waiters always work for real owners or managers. Amateurs may work for professionals, and notably do so in the trendier bars and brasseries of the Covent Garden-Soho triangle, but professionals will not work for amateurs. The truffled terrine of sweetbreads from the stripped pine kitchen of the Old Farmhouse may be out

CARE AND TRAINING OF WAITERS

of this world, but it will be served by a village girl straight out of Agatha Christie. (I once had the riveting experience of observing a not completely professional waitress tip an entire leg of lamb into the lap of the then Prime Minister. 'That's quite all right, my dear,' soothed the Rt Hon James Callaghan – for it was he – as the wretched girl stuttered her apologies – 'but could you take it back on your tray as it's quite hot?')

Real owners and real managers, with whom we may couple real maîtres d' or head waiters, have themselves as likely as not been real waiters in their day – trained, probably, in the family business. (Former chefs, curiously enough, however serious their sauces, are far less professional when they set up for themselves.) Certainly there will be no front-of-house task from emptying the ashtrays to serving a table for twelve which they cannot and have not done themselves. The real restaurant owner is never above replacing a dropped knife or changing a tablecloth. At the same time he has his own important job to do, which consists largely of having eyes in the back of his head. He can sense trouble a mile off and deal with it instantly, expertly and quietly. He is like the captain of a cruise liner. If the ship hits the rocks the responsibility is his and his alone, which is why he keeps a firm hand on the wheel.

But discarding metaphor, a real waiter does not need a firm hand and mutters about the restraints put upon him in the subterranean clubs where real waiters congregate after last orders (amateur waiters use jazz clubs). He is a self-starter.

A real waiter does not get flustered. Faced with what to the amateur is always the most amazing and unexpected and unprecedented and unnerving circumstance that the restaurant is what it was designed and intended and always yearned to be, ie, full, the real waiter is possessed by a confident, almost trance-like tranquility in which he is capable of anything short of levitation. It is one of the signs of a properly-run restaurant staffed by proper waiters that it is easier to get served when the room is full than when it is empty. Real waiters grow bored and listless when there is little for them to do, but are always full of beans when the action starts.

A real waiter can work out your bill without consulting the menu and tot it up without consulting a pocket calculator. He knows twelve and a half per cent of everything.

A real waiter is on to all the backstage tricks and dodges yet looks as if garlic butter wouldn't melt in his mouth.

A real waiter never looks as if his corns hurt or his mother is dead. A real waiter is neutral. He may be, in exceptional circumstances, a 'character' like the ultra-rude Herbie at Costello's Bar in New York, or the singing Alfredo at Kettner's, but that has to be by the indulgence of his clients.

One of the differences between amateur and professional waiters is that amateurs don't like to be addressed as 'Waiter!' (They often sport badges announcing their names as Dave or Debbie.) But I would never use the appellation to a professional waiter either, in the unlikely event that I could not attract his attention with the merest twiddle of a finger. The word, using all due respect, is 'Sir!'

Cloth Ears

A WAITER CAN EFFECTIVELY sabotage a meal simply by not listening to what is said to him.

'... And my guest would like a mixed salad with watercress if you have any, but no onion.'

'Yes sir, one mixed salad.'

'But without onion, and with watercress if there is any.'

Later:

'Waiter, my guest wanted a mixed salad with watercress but no onion. This has onion but no watercress.'

'I'll see if he has any, sir.'

'Thank you. But you are leaving my guest with a salad containing onion. She does not like onions. Would you please take this away and replace it with the mixed salad she ordered? And could it be a fresh salad, not this one with the onion picked off because it will still taste of onion?'

Later:

'Waiter, this is the same mixed salad you brought before, but with the onion removed. Could we have the fresh salad I ordered, please? And did you ask about the watercress?'

'I don't think there is any.'

'But would you find out? And could we have some oil and vinegar?'

'Vinaigrette.'

'No, oil and vinegar....'

The kind of inattention that might be shrugged off in the hullabaloo of a dinner party can turn a cosy lunch for two into a teeth-grinding experience. See *Troublemaking*.

Ugly Customers

IF THERE WERE a formal Guild of Lunch Companions, the following would stand a good chance of being stripped of their napkins and drummed out.

Those who –

– recommended a restaurant to the *Good Food Guide* with the reservation that the celery was too soggy;

– book and don't turn up (especially since some restaurants are so grateful for the courtesy of a cancellation phone call that when the absentee does finally make it for lunch they treat him like a favourite customer);

– arrive on spec and expect, as regulars, the people sitting at their usual table to be turfed off it;

– canoodle – or quarrel – to the embarrassment of neighbouring tables (canoodling or quarrelling to their amusement is all right);

– take it out on the waiter when the bad temper they're in is with each other;

– lie: eg, by pretending that the waiter has got the order wrong because they don't like the look of what he's brought, or that they booked a table when they didn't, or that they've been waiting twenty-five minutes for that drink when they've only been waiting ten (which, admittedly, does feel like twenty-five);

– talk loudly about the indifferent service;

– or, perhaps in what they believe to be justifiable exasperation, act as supernumerary waiters themselves, collecting chairs, ashtrays, menus, napkins, cruets and anything else they may be short of from other tables. (If they think they're being helpful, they should have a word with the waiter whose station they have just raided);

– get noisily drunk;

[95]

– demand the restaurant to live up to expectations it does not aspire to;

– ask for the manager when it is quite plain that the reason for the hiccup in the service is that the chef has just been carried out on a stretcher, followed by two policemen escorting a commis chef in handcuffs;

– lean over and chat to the people at the next table between courses, or even between mouthfuls;

– affect to be friends of the management, and threaten to write to the top man about some real or imagined slight;

– or worse, actually do so;

– question every item on the bill as if arraigning the waiter for fraud, and then when they can find nothing wrong, declare. 'Well, it still seems a ridiculous price for what we've had';

– engage the waiter in reminiscent conversation about how often they used to come here in the old days, when he is holding two armfuls of hot, but rapidly cooling, plates of food;

– talk to the staff with their mouths full (or to their guests, if it comes to that – but at least their guests can always walk out);

– ride roughshod over the restaurant's settling-up policy – eg, by refusing to abide by the cash-limit restriction they may put on payment by cheque (All right, the rule may be tiresome, and there's probably nothing they can do to a transgressor provided the cheque doesn't bounce, but it is after all their restaurant);

– after sending the waiter away with a flea in his ear, take the edge off their lunch companion's appetite by confiding, 'I'd have said a good deal more, but you know what they're supposed to do to the soup if they take against you, don't you?';

– carry on generally as if their own bad behaviour were an item to be charged and put on the bill (Perhaps it should be, without their knowledge. After all, the appalling John Fothergill of *An Innkeeper's Diary* notoriety did get away with charging some of his customers extra for being ugly.)

Smokeism

SMOKEISM IS THE righteous persecution of smokers by prigs. Though by now a thriving branch of local government and the civil service, smokeism was pioneered in the kind of country-based restaurant that gets long, gushing (though nit-picking) entries in the *Good Food Guide* – the type of place where the quail done with coriander has sometimes been not entirely up to scratch but is just about made up for by the passion-fruit cheesecake. Cigars and, ugh, pipes, have long been banished. Now all forms of smoking including the silkiest of Silk Cut are Corona non grata.

I have not myself smoked for eight years but I have eaten some of my best lunches in rooms blue with the smoke of Gauloises. This among dedicated eaters addressing themselves earnestly to the matter of lunch. Far from being insulted at the very idea of his concoctions being contaminated by smoke or his guests' palates by nicotine, the chef has taken every opportunity to step out of his kitchen for a quick fag.

Where the tables are close together and the cooking is serious, I don't mind an injunction not to smoke. I particularly don't mind because that is not the kind of restaurant I am likely to be in. If there is a comfortable annexe or lounge I am to be shuffled into for the coffee and brandy – another arrangement I don't care for, except in country house restaurants where it is all part of the act – then I would gladly hold off my cigar until then, if I still smoked cigars. But I don't want restaurants requesting me not to smoke any more than I want them to advise me to control my drinking or eat more green vegetables.

If smokeism is about health, lunch is not supposed to be healthy. It is healthier not to eat lunch at all.

If it's about ecology, smokeists should confine their

THE THEORY & PRACTICE OF LUNCH

zeal to vegetarian restaurants where the environment is not already polluted by the cooking in various ways of various animals.

If it's about gastronomic fastidiousness, I don't believe fastidious gastronomes go out for lunch anyway – they're far too mean, judging by their whingeing in the *Guide* about the places they have dinner in.

Lunch is not about stopping anybody doing anything. Ladies and gentlemen, you may smoke.

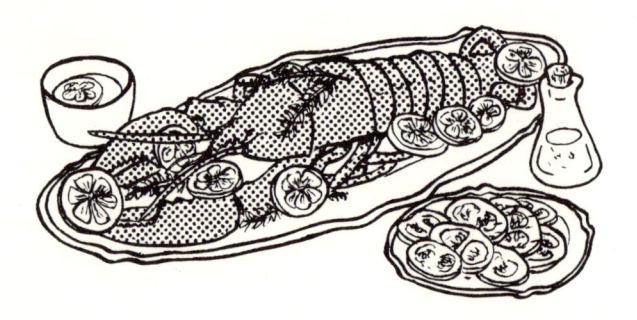

Why Are We Waiting?

*T*HOUGH LUNCH SHOULD be taken at leisure – three hours is about right – it should be at the lunch companions' leisure, not the restaurant's. If you have to click fingers or strive to catch eyes, you're in the wrong place.

The pace (a good maître d' will conduct his staff like an orchestra) has to be just so – not hurried, but not too unhurried either. I have known waiters come up so fast to enquire what we'd like for dessert that my lunch companion has replied, waxing satirical, 'Sorry to keep you waiting, but I still had my mouth full of potato.' But I have also known waiters – the same ones, on occasion – upon being asked 'Could you give us five minutes, please?' not to make a re-appearance for over half an hour, and then only in response to messages sent down the line.

Reasonable delays are pardonable, so long as you are left with something to drink (do not, if I have not said this already, and even if I have it cannot be stressed too strongly, ever let them place the wine out of reach), something to nibble at and something to look at, over and above the menu and each other. Unreasonable delays are unpardonable. By that I mean waiting forty-five minutes for a slice of melon, as I have done before now, while some kitchen topiarist finds time to serrate its edges in the form of a castle battlement. If for some unavoidable reason the service has gone completely haywire, it is up to the maître d' to come forward and explain that the kitchen is on fire at the moment. If the reason is avoidable – staff skiving or sulking, an order gone astray or

THE THEORY & PRACTICE OF LUNCH

congealing unnoticed – it is up to him to get it sorted out and apologise. In either case, he should give lunch companions a truthful estimate of how long they may expect to wait, so that they may judge whether to order another drink, or, better, accept one on the house.

My yardstick on the tolerability or otherwise of waiting for my lunch is the quantity of wine left in the bottle by the time the main course turns up. Half a bottle, and their timing is just about right. An empty bottle, and they've gone too far. Admittedly, since I tend to drink faster when agitated, the distance between those two criteria could be very slight indeed, but then time takes on a peculiarly elastic quality in restaurants. Five minutes without food or wine can seem like an hour. Yet an hour in good company goes like five minutes.

What restaurants can do to keep the service running smoothly is touched on elsewhere (see *Care and training of waiters*). But what can lunch companions themselves do to ensure that the meal – or absence of it – does not drag on interminably; or just as importantly, that it is not over so quickly as to induce a fit of hiccups?

The truth is that someone has to be in control of the situation. In perhaps seventy-five per cent of restaurants for perhaps ninety per cent of the time – and not all of them high-class places, by any means – it can safely be left in their hands. Otherwise, lunch companions themselves need to oil the wheels of the clattering gravy train.

The essence is in the ordering. Order your aperitif the moment you sit down, and ask for the menu. Should it not arrive at once, ask for it again. Do not, however, even open it until the aperitifs are on the table. Thereafter, the ordering should be done at the lunch companions' own pace. Do not be intimidated by the looming presence of a waiter sucking his pencil if you've yet to make up your minds – send him away to suck it at someone else. The briefest of nods, when you're ready, should signal him back. If he doesn't respond, tell the maître d' firmly that you'd like to order. (Once you've decided what you mean to have, by the way, it's not always a good idea to go on browsing idly through the menu, since many waiters –

[101]

in contrast with the pencil-sucking presence above – will assume that you're not yet ready for them.) When you do order, should the wine list not be produced at once, don't assume it will materialise in due course, but ask for it to be brought. If the first course arrives before the wine list, send it back. If it arrives before the wine (you will have buttonholed the sommelier and kept him waiting for your order rather than give him the chance to disappear again into his Ali Baba wine jar), do not touch a morsel until the bottle is on the table, opened. Should you wish for a second bottle, do not wait until your glasses are drained before asking for it. When you have finished your main course, refuse to enter into further negotiations as to pudding or cheese until you have digested it. When you are ready, signal as much. Do not be railroaded into having coffee before you want it, just to save the staff's shoeleather. Do not, if it is only just coming up to three, be hurried into asking for the bill by the sight of waiters laying tables for dinner.

All this may sound awfully bad for the digestion, but it is considerably less so than sitting fuming over a side-plate of breadcrumbs while there is slow-motion chaos all around you. And when it comes down to it, it is only a touch of the tiller we are talking about in most cases.

You are unlikely, anyway, to encounter the reception accorded me in the restaurant of the National Hotel in Leningrad some years ago when, after days had seemingly elapsed without even sight of a menu, I despatched my Intourist guide to complain about the service.

Another fortnight went by. Then the kitchen doors swung open and an alarming procession consisting of the chef flanked by all his kitchen staff marched purposefully in my direction. The way I tell it now, most of them were brandishing carving knives and cleavers, but that may be an embellishment. The rest is not.

The deputation arranged itself around my table and the chef addressed me through my guide. 'Upon receiving complain of guest, kitchen committee has met in emergency session in spirit of self-criticism. Kitchen committee has passed unanimous resolution calling for

WHY ARE WE WAITING?

improvements from all restaurant workers.' Since a response seemed called for, I made a short speech to the effect that we all had our off days, and the delegation trooped back to the kitchen. At last a waiter appeared and we asked for a menu. He shook his head regretfully. Lunch, he said, was off.

Troublemaking

I was in a Covent Garden restaurant once when a diner, to make a debating point with the management, rose to his feet, picked up his chair and smashed it to smithereens on the table.

I do not recommend this course of action to lunch companions. The point does come, however, when a protest has to be made. If the wine simply won't arrive and they've brought you veal instead of fish and your guest nothing whatever, a word is in order.

There is no point in sending for the manager because in the kind of place you're in, he won't come. Get up from your table and find him. Ask what is wrong and assess the possibility of its being put right in the forseeable future. If the man seems incompetent, uncaring or arrogant, pay for what you can be legitimately charged for, cut your losses, and leave. Then go directly to the restaurant you should have gone to in the first place, where you're guaranteed a good lunch – or, if you're in a strange town, to the place you would have gone to had the coin not come down tails – and start again. A bad lunch experience is like falling off a bicycle – you have to get on again at once before you lose your nerve.

But there is bad service and bad service. It is important not to make a fuss out of all proportion to the reason for it. Five years ago, to my subsequent regret, I stormed out of one of my neighbourhood restaurants over their insistence that I take my coffee at the bar so that they could give my table to a party they claimed had booked it. I was quite justified, but was it worth becoming an exile for, when there are so few good restaurants in my neck of the woods? No: and so after an interval I slunk back under a false name, which I have been using for

TROUBLEMAKING

my reservations there ever since. I'm quite sure they know my true identity but that they resolved early on to fall in with my little face-saving formula.

Nor is there any point in making a fuss because the standards of service are not that of the Ritz. (Unless, that is, the Ritz is where you happen to be lunching.) A restaurant can only live up to its own pretensions, not those of its customers. You may have high expectations, but if you do not see them on the menu, you have to take the place for what it is.

At dinner, when time is not of the essence, it is possible to get off to a bad start and survive it. Lunch has to go like clockwork from the beginning if it is to be a great success. That means that if things do start to go wrong, you have to decide whether to be magnanimous and not get upset over trifles – by far better for your digestion, if it's only a question of a forgotten butter knife and a waiter with a wall eye – or whether to risk your lunch going down like a failed soufflé by getting into a tizz.

There is a third course. As a general rule troublemaking is the function of the host, the guest being expected to pretend that nothing is less than perfect. But there does come a point when the service is so appalling that it cannot help but take over as the main talking-point between the besieged lunch companions; in which event they might as well sit back and enjoy it. It is still going to be a terrible lunch, but once they conspiratorially acknowledge that they are taking part in an episode of Fawlty Towers, they can save the day by gleefully anticipating what is going to go wrong next, unnerving the Manuel thinkalike by sending the salad back again and again and again until he has got it absolutely right, fetching the manager to the table and asking for suggestions as to what they might drink their wine out of, and so on. One pair of lunch companions I know operate like a Bonnie and Clyde hit team when they meet bad service, an eye signal from one to the other indicating when the time has come to take the sub-machine guns out of their violin cases. She is all sweet reason, he the heavy. Then they reverse roles and he is patience on a monument,

THE THEORY & PRACTICE OF LUNCH

she the termagant. Then they move in for the kill, in a sustained and concerted denunciation of the wretched establishment's shortcomings. Managements go white when they see them coming, but they always contrive to make the best of their lunch.

We're talking now, of course, about shambling ineptitude on an inspired scale. If the restaurant is just having an off-day, it should be let down lightly. If, however, the manager takes a superior attitude by coming the Basil Fawlty or treating genuine complainants as nitpicking nuisances, or if he takes the attitude, 'All right, we admit we've screwed it, but now you'll just have to make the best of a bad job,' then he needs to be jumped on from a great height.

I refuse to give a bad restaurant owner the satisfaction of not allowing me to pay for my disaster of a lunch. What can be a genuine gesture of regret where there has been a simple, self-acknowledged cock-up, is but a sneering strategy to have the last word in the context of a diabolical restaurant run by someone who ought to be doing something else for a living (and usually has been: nearly all truly awful restaurants are run by people who've failed at one profession and thought they'd found an easy touch worthy of their talents).

Having been served a memorably disastrous meal at a tarted-up village pub in the north-east – 'worth a detour' the local guidebook said: I didn't realise that they must have meant it was advisable to go round the village instead of through it – I asked for the manager to come forward and explain why I had had to wait for nearly an hour only to be given something utterly different from what I'd ordered, why the vegetables had never arrived at all, why the house white wine was served lukewarm, and why he had not emerged from his lair to sort things out after three SOS's from my table. Back came the waitress. The manager sent his apologies. Why didn't he bring his apologies personally? The waitress didn't know, but she had instructions to say that the bill was on the house.

'Tell your invisible manager,' I said, producing my

∽ TROUBLEMAKING ∾

credit card, 'that I only accept hospitality, even terrible hospitality, from people whom I have met.'

The waitress scuttled off and returned. 'He says he insists.'

'*I* insist,' I maintained. 'If I had the cash about me I should put it on the table and leave. As it is, I shall remain here until you bring me a credit card voucher to sign. Convey that to the absentee landlord.'

Once again the waitress took my credit card off for arbitration. 'He says if you found anything wrong with your lunch he'd rather you didn't pay for it, and that's that.'

'Tell him,' I said, arms folded, 'that if I am not allowed to settle my bill I shall call the police.'

That did it. The manager still didn't appear but the bill did. I paid for a dish I had not ordered and vegetables I had not had and left, the victor.

The Deserving Rich

THE WEEKEND IN Rome was supposed to be my reward for finishing a book. As we reached Heathrow I was already salivating in anticipation of the ravioli and gamberetti, or maybe the risotto and gamberi, at Mastrostefano on the Piazza Navona. Reaching the check-in desk I was trying to decide between the fruit tart and the *millefeuilles*. A moment later lunch in Rome had turned to ashes in my mouth. All flights cancelled: the air controllers were on strike.

As a child I was once lured to the dentist on the promise that I was being taken to the pantomine. The mixture of emotions I felt then – dismay, anger, disappointment and a sense of betrayal – was exactly reproduced as I trudged across to the bank and changed my lire back into pounds, preparatory to the dreary journey back to N1 and an afternoon watching racing on television.

My prospective lunch companion then had an inspired idea. The idea was lunch. We had set off to celebrate, and celebrate we would.

I made two phone calls – one to a couple of friends inviting them to join us for lunch, the other to the White Elephant reserving a table for four.

We commenced at noon with champagne cocktails. We concluded at three-thirty with a last round of Armagnacs. By the time we rolled out into Curzon Street I had blown every penny of the money earmarked for four meals in Rome. I do not remember exactly what we had after the caviar and chilled vodka – wild strawberries came into the proceedings somewhere – but I know we lunched like royalty (the chicken-leg-gnawing Tudors, that is, rather than the sparrow-pecking Windsors). A

THE DESERVING RICH

family of four could have lived for a week on what I paid but I did not, and do not, regret my profligacy for a second. It was the lunch to end all lunches – as famous a celebration as we would ever have had in Rome, with the added bonus that we didn't have to go through Customs at the end of it.

Spending a lot of money on meals comes hard to the British, which is one reason we ate so indifferently before the invention of the expense account. It still, to many, seems a crime to spend in restaurants what could more usefully and with more lasting benefit have been spent in stores or supermarkets.

To those who would sooner buy Premium Bonds than invest in lunch, I have nothing to say. They would presumably have no use for this book anyway, regarding it as not nearly as good value as a new nodding dog for the back windscreen of the Ford Escort. To dedicated lunch companions, I would plead that there is nothing wrong in a little wholesome extravagance from time to time, nor in occasionally squandering part of one's rainy day nestegg on a rainy day lunch (the best antidote ever devised against bad weather doldrums).

We are not talking about paying through the nose. Lunch in a blatantly overpriced restaurant is never a very happy experience: even though one may not be footing the bill oneself, the occasion is laced with irritation at being taken for a mug, plus guilt at the wanton waste of money. What we are talking about is living high off the hog from time to time. If the lunch genuinely seems worth the price of a good pair of shoes, there should be no qualms about shelling out for it. Nor should there be any self-flagellation afterwards at having nothing tangible to show for the money. The memory of a good lunch with a favourite lunch companion is every bit as lasting as the pair of shoes you didn't buy, and unlike them it will never let in water.

On the expense of lunch in general, just as members of some religious sects and political extremists put aside a certain proportion of their income for the cause, I reckon each true lunch companion should fix a tithe which is to be spent exclusively on lunch. Not eating lunch out of some financial consideration such as saving up to go on holiday can be a perilous habit to get into (a worse one is accepting lunch invitations but never reciprocating them).

Lunch should be regarded as one of the basic necessities of life like fuel and clothing. Indeed, were I in charge of compiling the cost of living index, it would include the price of two lunches a week at a decent Italian restaurant.

The Deserving Poor

But what if one simply can't afford to eat out? I do not wish to sound like Lady Bountiful instructing the labouring classes on how they may nourish themselves for a week on a knuckle of veal and some lentils, but I would maintain that in general the only people who cannot afford to eat out are those who would never eat out even if they could afford it.

Eating in is certainly more economical (I recommend Charles Elme Francatelli's *A Plain Cookery Book For The Working Classes*, published in 1852, whose recipe for baked cod's head carries the footnote 'A few oysters would be an improvement'. They would, wouldn't they?) and it can be rollicking good fun (see *Home cooking*). But eating out makes a nice change from boil-in-the-bag. And it is possible on the tightest of budgets.

Students manage to eat out hugely on their grants. This is not because their grants are large but because their appetites are. They go Chinese, Indian or Greek and order the cheapest, most plentiful and most filling dishes on the menu, washed down with rough wine. (They insist on believing, though, that any Chinese joint where the Chinese themselves eat has to be good. Myth.)

The notoriously unwell-off bedsitter brigade contrive to eat out quite a lot too. Takeaways may be cheaper, but there is not a lot of atmosphere in a TV dinner.

Both groups being consumers of only one square meal a day, augmented by snacks, they do tend to dine out rather than lunch out when funds permit. They should reverse the rule occasionally, particularly at weekends when they have time to indulge themselves even if they have little money to do it on (the dictum that going Dutch

THE THEORY & PRACTICE OF LUNCH

is not True Lunch, by the way, is waived in the case of the deserving poor).

Dinner, in these circumstances, is too often a question of mere Nosh – eating because having had little all day, one feels hungry. Enjoying the occasion can be a secondary consideration. An impetuously-planned lunch, however, is always an exhilarating experience. One is not only feeding the inner man but refreshing the parts dinner cannot reach. Lunch gives uplift.

As to where lunch may economically be taken, neighbourhood restaurants are usually a good bet, and the best neighbourhood restaurants are Greek or Italian. Earl's Court where I live is not known as Salmonella Junction for nothing, but we do have two first-class Italian restaurants in Bistro Benito in the Earl's Court Road, and La Primula across the street from my house. They both exude jollity as Italian places so often do, and they have given me many a sprawling family lunch without breaking the bank. Some of the local Chinese and Indian restaurants may be cheaper, but I always see them as dinner places. (And beware Designer Indian – flash and expensive.)

If we are talking about sheer value for money, however, the Pizza Express chain cannot be beaten. I have said that taking the kids to a pizza palace may be jolly but it does not constitute lunch. Nor does it: but swopping slices of Margharita and Venezia over a bottle of something crisp and white in the light and elegant surroundings of a Pizza Express is something else again, and you can do it for well this side of a fiver a head.

If the deserving poor have credit cards they should always use this means of paying, not only because it staves off the debt for another day but in the hope of the voucher going astray – a fat chance admittedly. It has happened to me only once – not, as you might imagine, in some hopelessly disorganised part of the world such as southern Italy (when in fact you find that the credit card account for meals consumed in the remotest of mountain villages is always waiting on the doormat on your return home), but in super-efficient America, where

℘ THE DESERVING POOR ℘

a few years ago my lunch companion and I got through about £80-worth of brunch at the classy Top of the Mark at the Mark Hopkins Hotel, and the bill did not filter through until fluctuations in the currency rate had lopped about £20 off the bill, some six months later. By then, of course, I had completely forgotten that I owed the money at all, and so I accepted the discount with rather less than good grace.

So much for the deserving poor's lunch when they are dipping into their own pockets (or lunching now and paying later). Now what about metaphorical rich uncles – in other words, accepting hospitality from friends more well-heeled than themselves? Should rich companions invite poor companions to the Savoy Grill, and if so, should the poor companions accept?

The case against both inviting and accepting is that the rich may seem to be showing off, while the poor may feel out of their depth, and subsequently will not feel happy reciprocating at some humble trattoria. The case in favour is that the rich should not discriminate between those who can afford to eat as well as they do and those who cannot, that their guests will be treated like lords if the Savoy Grill is indeed the venue, and that just as much as the Savoy is a treat for the poor lunch companion, the humble trattoria will in due course make a nice change for the rich lunch companion. The ayes, I think, have it.

Besides, what the deserving poor deserve most is a slap-up lunch.

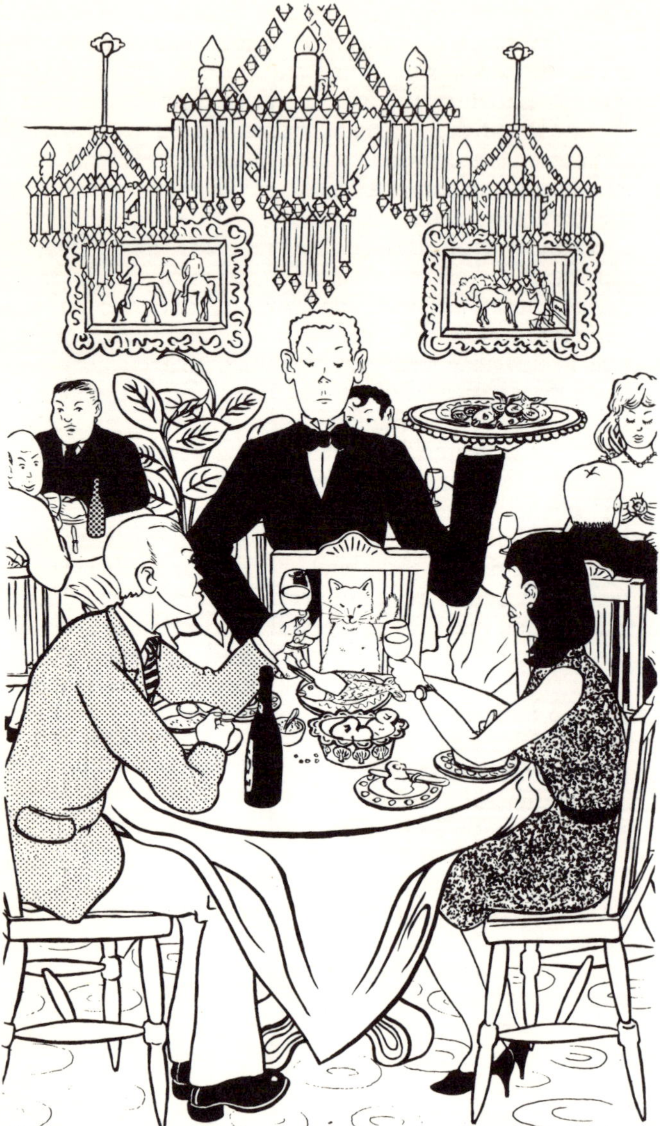

Fifty Uses Of Lunch

To propose an affair (but not a marriage – that's a dinner engagement).
To conduct an affair.
To end an affair.
To celebrate good news.
To cauterise bad news.
To catch up on gossip.
To spread rumours.
To rubbish the boss.
To have a really good row.
To kiss and make up.
To avoid work.
To fight a depression.
To make plans.
To hold an inquest.
To explore a relationship.
To mark an anniversary.
To defy doctor's orders.
To reward oneself.
To start off a holiday.
To round off a holiday.
To exchange presents.
To seal a friendship.
To delay Christmas shopping.
To celebrate the cat's birthday.
To get out of the house.
To spoil oneself.
To say thank you.
To say please.
To seek a refuge.
To see how an ex is getting on.

THE THEORY & PRACTICE OF LUNCH

To see what happens.
To charge one's batteries.
To ask advice.
To prelude a diet.
To end a diet.
To live dangerously.
To live vicariously.
To find an ally.
To have one's confidence restored.
To bolster someone else's.
To be irresponsible.
To be in the swim.
To get back in the swim.
To seduce someone.
To say sorry.
To make someone happy.
To make whoopee.
To relax.
To anticipate bed.
        or
For the hell of it.

Bon appetit!

The Good Mood Guide

As I have said more than once, this is not a food guide and I am not in the business of recommending restaurants. The places listed here are those mentioned in the book for one reason or another. The food at some is better than at others – that said, I offer no judgements. Some might suit the reader's taste, not to mention the reader's pocket – some might not. What all have in common is that I have lunched (or in two cases dined) uncommonly well in them by the yardstick that the experience has put me in a good mood for the rest of the day.

The few blank pages that follow are for your own favourites. And remember the true lunch companion's rule – if you find a good restaurant, pass it on, unless you have a sentimental or prudent reason for hogging it to yourself.

ALGONQUIN HOTEL, 59 West 44th Street, New York, NY 10036 (212 840 6800)

BISTRO BENITO, 166 Earl's Court Road, London SW5 (01 373 6646)

BOX TREE RESTAURANT, Church Street, Ilkley, W. Yorks (0943 608484) *Dinner only*

LA BRASSERIE, 272 Brompton Road, London, SW3 (01 584 1688)

CAFÉ PELICAN, 45 St Martin's Lane, London WC2 (01 379 0309)

CAFÉ ROYAL GRILL ROOM, 68 Regent Street, London W1 (01 437 9090)

THE THEORY & PRACTICE OF LUNCH

CHEZ VICTOR, 45 Wardour Street, London W1
(01 437 6523)

COSTELLO'S BAR, 225 East 44th St., New York, NY
10017 (212 599 9614)

LA COUPOLE, 102 Boulevard Montparnasse, Paris 14e
(331 43201420)

ENGLISH'S OYSTER BAR AND SEAFOOD
RESTAURANT, 29/31 East Street, Brighton
(0273 27980)

L'EPICURE, 28 Frith Street, London W1 (01 437 2829)

L'ESCARGOT, 48 Greek Street, London W1
(01 437 2679)

L'ETOILE, 30 Charlotte Street, London W1 (01 636 7189)

LA FAVORITA, Parrucchiano, Corso Italia, Sorrento,
Naples (39 81 878 1321)

FISHERMAN'S WHARF, 15 The Side, Newcastle Upon
Tyne (0632 321057) *Dinner only*

FREDERICK'S, Camden Passage, London N1
(01 359 2888)

GEALE'S FISH RESTAURANT, 2 Farmer Street,
London W8 (01 727 7969)

THE GROUCHO CLUB, 45 Dean Street, London W1
(01 439 4685) *Members only*

GRAVETYE MANOR, West Hoathly, East Grinstead,
W. Sussex (0342 810 567)

HUNGRY HORSE, 196 Fulham Road, London SW10
(352 7757)

JOE ALLEN, 13 Exeter Street, London WC2
(01 846 0651)

THE GOOD MOOD GUIDE

JULES BAR, 85 Jermyn Street, London SW1
(01 930 4700)

KETTNERS, 29 Romilly Street, London W1 (01 437 6437)

LANGAN'S BAR AND GRILL, 7 Down Street, London
W1 (01 491 0990)

LANGAN'S BRASSERIE, Stratton House, Stratton Street,
London W1 (01 493 6437)

LOCANDA CIPRIANI, Isoladi Torcello, Venice
(39 41 730 150)

MANZI'S SEAFOOD RESTAURANT, 1 Leicester
Street, London WC2 (01 724 0224)

MERIDIANA, 169 Fulham Road, London SW3
(01 589 8815)

MIRABELLE, 56 Curzon Street, London W1
(01 499 1940)

MARK HOPKINS' INTER-CONTINENTAL (The
Mark), 1 Nob Hill, San Francisco, California, CA 94108
(415 392 3434)

MASTROSTEFANO, 94 Piazza Romana, Rome
(39 6 541 669)

NEAL STREET RESTAURANT, 26 Neal Street, London
WC2 (01 836 8368)

OYSTER BAR, Grand Central Station, New York City
(212 490 6650)

POLO LOUNGE, The Beverly Hills Hotel, 9641 Sunset
Boulevard at Beverly Drive, Los Angeles (213 276 2251)

PIZZA EXPRESS, Various locations throughout London
and the South. Head office: 29 Wardour Street, London
W1 (01 437 7215)

PONTEVECCHIO, 256 Old Brompton Road, London
SW5 (01 373 9082)

THE THEORY & PRACTICE OF LUNCH

LA PRIMULA, 12 Kenway Road, London SW5
(01 370 5958)

THE RITZ, Piccadilly, London W1 (01 493 8181)

SAVOY GRILL ROOM, Strand, London WC2
(01 836 4343)

SOHO BRASSERIE, 23/25 Old Compton Street, London
W1 (01 439 9301)

LA TERRAZZA, 16 Greek Street, Leeds (0532 432880)

LE TRAIN BLEU, Gare de Lyon, Paris 12ᵉ (331 434 0906)

THE TRAFALGAR, 40 North Albert Street, Fleetwood
(03917 2266)

VAL CENO, 143 Fleet Street, London EC4 (01 353 9559)

WALDORF ASTORIA, 301 Park Avenue at 50th Street,
New York, NY 10022 (212 355 3000)

WHEELER'S THREE LITTLE ROOMS, 17 Market
Street, Brighton, E. Sussex (0273 25135)

WHEELER'S SHERIDAN HOTEL, 64 King's Road,
Brighton, E. Sussex (0273 23221)

WHITE ELEPHANT CLUB, 28 Curzon Street, London
W1 (01 499 2763) *Members only*

WIG AND PEN CLUB, 229 Strand, London WC2
(01 353 1262) *Members only*